TRAMP STEAMER

and

THE SILVER BULLET

Jeffrey Kelly

TRAMP STEAMER

and

THE SILVER BULLET

Houghton Mifflin Company Boston 1984

Library of Congress Cataloging in Publication Data

Kelly, Jeffrey, 1946–
Tramp Steamer and the Silver Bullet.

Summary: The adventures and misadventures of two boys,
Tramp and Silver, as they become involved with haunted
houses, eccentric ladies, spiders, meat-eating plants,
and secret tunnels.
1. Children's stories, American. [1. Friendship—
Fiction. 2. Mystery and detective stories. 3. Humorous
stories.] I. Title.
PZ7.K2962Tr 1984   [Fic]   84-15668
ISBN 0-395-36632-1

Printed in the United States of America

s 10 9 8 7 6 5 4 3 2 1

For Sarah and Rebecca

Contents

TRAMP STEAMER
and
THE SILVER BULLET

1
"Ghouls!"

"GHOULS!"

"That's right, ghouls," said The Silver Bullet. "Cold as bloodsuckers, ugly as warts, mean as a mouthful of razor blades, which is just about what they have for teeth — razor blades!"

What a gruesome description — fantastic, impossible — could it be true? Just like The Silver Bullet to try to rattle my bones in the dead of a dreary dark night. What was I doing here, anyway? Face down on my belly in some cold, weedy lot, at the end of a dead end street, listening to stories about ghouls and razor blades, while a family of beetles used my head for a trampoline. What had I gotten myself into this time?

"Where do you suppose these . . . ghouls come from?" I asked, not at all sure I wanted to know.

"I don't suppose," said Silver. "I *know* they come from the cemetery. Every Halloween night they open up the graves, pull out the coffins, and look around for places to hide. Like inside that house, over there."

He pointed across the street, at a dilapidated, two-story house set behind an iron gate and a high stone wall. The house had a boarded-up appearance, a sagging roof, and a broken-down porch that looked as if a huge bite had been taken out of one end. A FOR SALE sign stuck up in the middle of a yard grown over with weeds and leaves and debris — an enormous trash heap.

"Nobody's been in there for years," I said.

"Nobody you know," said Silver.

"What makes you so sure?"

The moon cast a sparkle in his eyes. "I've seen them," he said. "Climbing over the stone wall, carrying the coffins they'd robbed on their backs. It was a couple of years ago, but I remember. You don't forget something like that. It was a night like tonight — cold and dark, the moon in and out of the clouds. Me hiding here all alone, freezing cold, not believing my eyes."

"What'd you do?"

"I waited 'til I figured out what they were up to. When I heard a window smash and saw smoke coming out of the chimney, I made my move. I climbed over the wall, snuck up to the front porch, and looked in a window. The shade was pulled down, but it had a hole in it, so there was no problem."

"Well?"

"Well what?"

"What'd you see?"

He leaned closer and spoke to me in an urgent whisper. "I saw ghouls," he said. "Six, seven, maybe more. Fiercely ugly. Some of them without faces. All eyes and teeth. Heads swollen, fat as pumpkins, only purple — bruised looking. You'll never guess what they were doing."

I shook my head.

"Dancing," he said. "They'd lit a fire in the fireplace, under a huge kettle ready to burst with boiling. They dragged the kettle into the center of the room and began to dance around it, slow motion–like, to some weird chant I couldn't understand. I tell you, I was scared."

"But what was in the kettle?"

He hesitated. A shadow crossed his face. "I don't know," he said. "Not for sure. Something to eat, I suppose. I heard a noise behind me — footsteps — and I got out of there fast."

His story over, Silver turned his attention back to the abandoned house. I watched him out of the corner of my eye. I was hoping for that dazzling smile of his to light up his face, or to hear him laugh out loud, something to assure me that he had everything under control. That he was just testing my courage, as he was apt to do. That he'd made it all up.

No smile came. His face was a frown. I'd never seen him looking so troubled, so lacking in confidence.

"Why didn't you tell me about all this before?" I asked him.

He ignored the question. "Come on," he said. "Once and for all, we're going to find out what's going on inside that house."

2
Hunters on Broomsticks

TRAMP STEAMER — THAT'S ME. IT'S A STRANGE NAME,
I agree, but when your last name is Steamer what nick-
name comes to mind? My real name is Stearns Obediah
Steamer, so you see the problem. My little sister, Ginger, calls me Pole, on account of my overall appearance,
which is tall and rangy (a nicer word than skinny). You
might say that my most outstanding characteristics are
things that aren't. My ears don't stick out, my feet
aren't abnormal, I don't smell. I happen to be good at
sports. I like to read. I spend a lot of time flexing the
muscles in my turtlelike neck to try to make them
larger. Pretty average stuff for a twelve-year-old. Or so
I'm told.

It was rainy after school, a Friday, the day of Halloween. I headed straight for The Silver Bullet's house. He
was home from boarding school, had sent me a postcard
telling me that he had something special planned for the
occasion. Of that I had no doubt. Halloween was Silver's favorite night of the year. When we were younger, he called it "hunting on broomsticks."

I should explain. For most of the neighborhood kids,
those who weren't "hunters," Halloween was just another night of trick or treating, a bag of candy, a squirt

of shaving cream, a silly prank or two. For those who were "hunters," such as Silver and myself, Halloween was no ordinary night at all. It was magic and devilry, and not the little kid kind. "We hunters seek trouble," Silver used to say, "or trouble seeks us. I prefer the former." He also preferred company on his Halloween excursions, that of his best friend and neighbor — me.

"Come on in!" Silver shouted. "And shut the door behind you."

I did. Gladly, for the rain was coming down hard now and had soaked through my sweater and shirt, right down to my underwear. The sounds of thunder boomed overhead. Once inside, I pulled off my soaking shoes and socks and kicked them up against the radiator. Silver was nowhere to be seen.

"I'll be right out." His voice came from inside the hideaway. "I'm fixing my flashlight. We've got something important to talk about."

I flopped down on the sofa and waited, feeling my body sink into the spongy cushions, the familiar loose spring uncoil and poke against my side. I couldn't say how many times I'd sat, bounced, wrestled, lain, even slept on that sofa. Probably thousands.

Silver had a wonderful room. For one thing, you could enter or leave it as you pleased, without having to go through the main part of the house, without ever seeing an adult, if you know what I mean. The room had its own private door, which opened onto the backyard.

Then there were Silver's possessions, and not the kinds of things your parents might buy for you. The three stuffed crows, for instance. Or his barrels of "collections": baseball cards, test tubes, bottle caps and batteries, cabbage-sized balls of string, and a smaller barrel full of Indian head nickels. Or the miniature refrigerator that he'd found at the dump, fixed himself, and kept full of salami and cream soda, his favorite food and drink. He even had a workbench piled high with tools and gadgets, including an electric popcorn popper and a ham radio set.

In addition, there was a rumpled bed, a ratty table you could put your feet on, a dresser (every drawer open), a stereo, and a poster of a light bulb superimposed on the face of Thomas Edison, with the caption "Got any bright ideas?" Two old-fashioned radiators stood hissing on opposite sides of a floor strewn with dirty laundry, an assortment of shoes, and enough dirty magazines to keep a guy going forever.

Perhaps best of all, behind an inconspicuous door beneath the stairs leading to the rest of the house, was the "hideaway," a windowless crawlspace just big enough for the two of us and the vegetable crate we used as a table. It was our secret meeting place, known only to Silver and myself, his father, and maybe to Mrs. Blanchard, his aunt, who looked after him when his father was away on business, which was a lot. Silver maintained that the hideaway was really the entrance to an escape tunnel built during the Civil War and since destroyed. I had no reason to doubt him.

It was a moment or two before the familiar mess of silver hair emerged, followed by a round, macaroni-colored face, a stout body, and a pair of surprisingly skinny legs. Some kid had once described Silver (not to his face) as an ostrich egg with roots. The description fit perfectly.

"Just the man I wanted to see," he said, scrambling to his feet. He was holding his flashlight, one with a wide, powerful beam. "Special night," he said with a chuckle. "Are you with me?"

"I thought I'd go trick or treating," I said half-jokingly.

The smile on his face became a frown. He gave a shrug and began to move about the room, puzzling over this and that, pretending not to notice me. Though a year older and in the eighth grade, Silver was considerably shorter than I, maybe by as much as three or four inches. But he more than made up for this deficiency — if that's what it was — by weighing more, being twice as fast (his weird silver hair and his speed afoot earned him his nickname), twice as strong, and at least twice as sly. It was unbelievable the way he could get me to do things that I might otherwise not have done, knowing the trouble I'd find myself in if I did.

"Suit yourself," he said at last. "By the way, who's going with you, your kid sister?"

"No," I practically shouted getting up from the couch. "I'll go by myself. If I go, that is. And I won't be wearing any costume either, so don't bother bringing it up."

"I won't," he said. "It's just . . ."

"Just what? What's wrong with candy on Halloween?"

He stopped fiddling with some metal gadget he'd

picked up off the workbench and looked at me. His dark eyes narrowed beneath two shaggy silver eyebrows. The muscles in his face became taut. He gave a nervous tug at a loose strand of hair behind his ear. When he spoke, it was in his most serious voice.

"Nothing," he said, "unless . . . there's more important business at hand."

"Like what?"

He sighed. "Anyone trick or treating with his kid sister wouldn't be interested," he said.

"Tell me," I said. "I can always change my mind."

"No," he said. "Besides, it could be dangerous."

He had me. "Tell me," I said. "Come on."

"Come by tonight, if you want to know," he said. "After it's dark and all the little kids have stopped ringing doorbells and have gone home for the night. Around nine o'clock. Wear dark clothes, bring a flashlight. And don't tell anyone where you're going."

"Where are we going?"

"You'll find out when we get there."

"I'll be here at eight-thirty," I said. "In case we want to leave early."

Silver looked at me and laughed, an infectious laugh, like the sound of bells ringing on an ice cream truck. A smile lit up his face. His eyes glowed with anticipation. "Tramp, my friend and fellow hunter," he said, "get ready for a night you'll never forget."

Unfortunately for the two of us, he was right.

3
A Bottle Full of Courage

HE WAS OFF AND MOVING, CROUCHED IN THE TALL grass, the wet leaves crunching beneath him. Overhead, the moon went behind some clouds. The night had become quiet, the rain slack, the wind still. In less time than it takes to crack a knuckle, The Silver Bullet was gone.

"Silver!" I called out. "Wait for me."

I followed his zigzag path through the grass, crawling on all fours as fast as I could. It took an anxious moment or two for me to catch up to him. He'd stopped to push aside a clump of grass, to get a better look at the iron-gate entrance to the abandoned house. I looked over his shoulder. The gate, partially illuminated by a nearby street lamp, was tightly secured by a chain and padlock. The gate must've been at least fifteen feet high, impossible to climb, with a row of spearlike prongs at the top.

"We can't climb that," I said.

"We don't have to. We can get in the same way the ghouls and I got in the last time. Over there."

He made a motion with his hand. A short distance away, a boulder the size of a Volkswagen had been pushed up against the stone wall, beneath a thick branch of an oak tree, which had grown over the wall from the inside.

"Here's the plan," said Silver. "We'll use that branch to swing up on top of the wall and drop down on the other side. Once we're both inside, we'll make our way along the wall toward the side of the house. There's a clump of trees near there where we can hide. Can you do it?"

I had a sudden thought. "Silver," I said, "if you didn't see what was inside the kettle, how do you know they're ghouls?"

Again he hesitated before answering. "I said I didn't know for sure. I saw something, but only for a second. Something that scared me worse than the footsteps I heard behind me. It happened when they were dragging the kettle into the center of the room. One of them stumbled, the kettle tipped sideways, and all the water or whatever it was sloshed to one side. It was then that I saw it, sticking up — but only for a second — before it sank back into the steaming liquid. I'm not positive, not at all, but it looked like . . . are you sure you want to know?"

I nodded, not at all sure.

"A human hand."

I was too stunned to speak. Silver was a great one for playing pranks, making up stories, lying through his teeth — but not to me, his best friend. He'd stretch the truth from time to time, but I could always tell when he had because he couldn't keep from smiling, from laughing out loud. Only this time he wasn't smiling or laughing. Not at all. And me having stupidly forgotten my flashlight.

"What do I do if I see one?" I asked.

"Simple," he said. "Make an *x* sign with your thumbs and say the chant to scare the dead away: 'Crossed thumbs, see the dead run.' "

"That's kid stuff," I said.

"Then don't do it," he said impatiently. "See what happens."

Rising to his knees, he slipped the knapsack he was carrying off his shoulders. The weatherbeaten canvas bag was as familiar to me as if it were my own. Rarely did Silver make a move without it, certainly not on a night like tonight. Of its bulky contents — extra bulky tonight — I could only guess, save the "safeguards" he always carried: knife, flashlight, matches, first-aid kit, compass, canteen, and, last of all, a salami sandwich.

"Here," he said, rummaging around inside the knapsack and pulling out a small bottle. "Take a swig of this. It'll give you courage."

I turned the bottle around in my hands. The label read CREAM SODA.

"Cream soda will give me courage?" I said doubtfully.

"It's not what it says," he said, giving me a look. "It's a potion I concocted myself, special for tonight. Try it."

I unscrewed the cap and put the bottle to my nose. Disgusting! Sewage and sweatsocks. I held the bottle as far away from my face as I could.

"Is it whiskey?" I asked him.

For the first time that night Silver smiled. "No," he said. "Though that would've worked as well. It's supposed to ward off evil spirits. I read about it in the same book I found the chant to scare the dead away."

"What's in it?"

"Believe me, you wouldn't want to know. Nothing poisonous. Just some stuff I found around the house. Give it here."

He took the bottle out of my hand, held his nose, and took a quick swallow.

"Awful!" he said, grimacing. "But worth it if it works. Sure you don't want some?"

"No, thanks," I said.

"Okay by me," he said. "But you keep the bottle in your pocket. It might come in handy later."

He was on the move again, crouched in the grass along the side of the road, with me trailing behind — right behind. Above us, like a watchful eye, the moon slipped out from behind the clouds, filling the road with shadows. The smell of burning leaves was in the air. I could hear the wind blowing in the treetops, the slow creaking of a rusty gate, and, though it could've been my imagination, the faraway sound of glass breaking.

Under my breath, so that Silver couldn't hear me, I repeated the chant to scare the dead away. "Crossed thumbs, see the dead run."

4
Candlelight!

SILVER WAS RIGHT. CLIMBING OVER THE WALL proved to be no problem at all. Once there, we headed in a roundabout way for the clump of trees he'd spoken about, where we could stay well hidden and keep a watch out for any peculiar goings-on. Was that the plan? I still didn't know exactly what Silver had in mind, but whatever it was I was sure to be in the middle of it, like it or not. And so what if my heart was pounding like a jackhammer?

About halfway there, Silver startled me by stopping short.

"Did you see that?" he whispered.

"See what?"

"The light. Inside the house. The flickering light."

"I . . . I didn't see anything."

"Left-hand window, next to the porch."

I braved a look. Across the yard, past the crooked FOR SALE sign, the house looked like a gigantic black shadow against the moonlit sky.

"I don't see anything," I said, relieved.

"It's gone now. Keep your eyes open."

A moment later, making our way across the hard ground, we reached the clump of trees — our destination. Only it wasn't. I didn't even have time to catch my breath.

"See that downstairs window, the one nearest us?" said Silver. "Follow me."

"But Silver . . ." I protested.

Too late. He was off and running, a silver cat in the moonlight.

"Here's what I want you to do," he whispered, when I was again by his side. "Go around front and give that door a bang like —"

"What! Why me?"

"Keep your voice down!"

"Why me?" I repeated.

"I'll stay here," he said, "and watch through this window. There's bound to be a commotion inside when you bang on the door."

"Yeah," I agreed. "Coming right for me."

"Stupid. Don't just stand there. Jump back into the bushes."

His abrasive manner was beginning to get to me. "Why don't *I* watch the window," I said stubbornly, "while *you* knock on the door?"

He regarded me silently. When he spoke it was in a softer voice than before.

"Your eyesight isn't as good as mine, Tramp. Besides, I know what to look for."

He was right. His eyesight was extraordinary. And he had been the one to see the ghouls, hadn't he? His plan made sense, but . . . oh!

He was pushing me, gently. "Go on, Tramp. You can do it."

At the front of the house, before a row of overgrown bushes that led to the porch, I stopped to look back. "Go on," Silver said. "I'll be here, waiting for you."

I got down on all fours and hacked my way through the wiry mesh of bushes until I felt my outstretched hand strike the underside of the porch. I took a gulp of air, managed to vault the railing, ran up to the front door, and . . .

BANG! BANG! BANG!

The echo of my efforts boomed like thunderclaps. Crack a knuckle and I was gone, nose-diving into the bushes, back along the same path I'd come, but a hundred times as fast.

Silver was barely able to contain himself. "I saw candlelight!" he said, practically shouting. "Look for yourself."

I was a tangle of arms and legs, face down in the dirt at his feet. Hauling me up by the collar, he pushed my nose against the glass, stepped back, and waited.

"I don't see a thing," I said, once I'd caught my breath. "There's a shade pulled down on the other side."

"There's a shade on every window," said Silver. "Look along the crack at the edge."

I did. "All I see is shade," I said.

He leaped forward and grabbed my arm. "Look there!" he demanded. "Off to the left. A smoking yellow flame, reflecting on the wall."

Then I, too, saw it. Or thought I did. It may have been the light from the distant street lamp, moonlight, or . . .

"Let's get out of here," I said.

But then a strange thing happened. By chance, I saw Silver's reflection in the window. I wasn't sure, but I could've sworn that he was smiling. I spun around to get a look, but in that instant the expression on his face had changed.

"Leave?" he said, deadly serious. "Why, Tramp, we hunters have just begun."

5
The Crack in the Window

BACK OF THE HOUSE WAS AN EVEN DARKER HALLOW-een night than in front. There was no street lamp to light a murky way, no narrow road, no open space for the moon to illuminate. Just the night and the edge of a forest that pressed in close to the house.

For the first time that night, Silver took out his flashlight and switched on the powerful beam. "Try the bottom windows," he said. "I'll check the door."

"Check it for what?"

"Don't play dumb with me," he said, pulling at the doorknob. "There's got to be a way to get inside."

I grabbed the sleeve of his jacket. "Inside?"

"Yeah," he said. "Hey-o! I think I've found it."

He had. The beam of his flashlight had settled upon a small window set high off the ground, almost hidden behind a row of tall bushes. Like sharp teeth, a splintery hole in the glass marked the bottom frame. In an instant, Silver had pulled away from me, raised the window, and hoisted himself and his knapsack up and in.

"Come on," he said, sticking his head out. "I'll give you a hand."

I shook my head. "Act crazy if you want to, Silver, but count me out."

"You're leaving?"

His question threw me. The thought of going home alone hadn't occurred to me.

"N-no," I stammered, "but . . ."

"Good," he said. "Because I'd sure feel safer if you came with me."

I couldn't abandon my friend now, could I?

"Okay." I agreed reluctantly. "But only as far as —"

"Whatever you say," he said. "Only, hurry. I don't want to spend any more time in here than necessary."

Before I knew it, I was standing in a small rectangular room that smelled of moldy wood, cast eerily aglow in the white light of Silver's flashlight. On either side of us, lining the walls, were rows of empty shelves.

"It's a —" I started to say "pantry," when Silver put a finger to his lips.

"Listen."

I listened and heard as he did the strange sounds coming from beneath us. Thud, scraaaape. Thud, scraaaape. Thud, thud, thud. A slow, rhythmic cadence, like someone — something — descending a flight of stairs.

"Sure you're not coming?" asked Silver.

I could feel my body break out in a rash of goose bumps. "I'll wait here," I said. "Don't be long."

He gave my shoulder a reassuring pat and said, "If anything happens, make a run for it. The hideaway. I'll meet you there."

In an instant he was gone, through an open door and into what appeared to be a narrow hallway — gone!

It was dark — very dark — and as cold as could be. I was shivering. In my mind, I pictured the steaming kettle and the hand of some poor person who'd met his boiled-lobster end. Or had he already been dead? Didn't ghouls rob graves? Wasn't that what the coffins were all about?

With a start, I remembered the bottle in my pocket. Silver had said that a swig would give me courage. I pulled the bottle out, unscrewed the lid, and, before I knew what I was doing, swallowed the entire syrupy contents in a single gulp. Yeatch! What vomit!

"Silver!" I shouted.

He didn't answer.

"Silver!"

I took a step forward, then another, into the hallway, where I stopped — cold. There it was, around a corner, no more than a dozen feet away — the yellow reflection of a flickering light, shadows dancing on a wall.

"Crossed thumbs, see the dead run," I squeaked.

The light dimmed, the shadows grew faint.

"Crossed thumbs, see the dead run!"

I urged myself on. If there'd been any danger, surely it would've come crashing down on top of Silver and me by now. But candlelight? Shadows?

One look and the mystery would be solved. What

else besides a yellow candle awaited me around the corner? One look and I'd know.

6
Hunters, Orange and Black

I WAS RUNNING. BLINDLY, IN THE DARK, MY LEGS AND arms pumping, I was running like I'd never run before. Back down the hallway, nose first out the pantry window — what a leap! — and into the woods behind the house, a thick woods of bare branches and tentaclelike roots that tore at my clothes and skin and seemed ready to grab hold of me. Down a steep embankment, knee-deep in freezing cold water, out again and scrambling up the bank on the other side. Faster I ran. Faster.

Then, before I knew it, I'd fallen, tripped over a rotten log that lay unseen across my path. Oooff! Flat on my stomach, the wind knocked out of me, my head banging the ground. Round and round I spun in a dizzying orbit.

Suddenly, with a bewildered shout, I leaped to my feet. The image of what I'd seen snapped into place. A snarling beast hunched down behind the flickering light of a yellow candle. A beast with a hideous head the size of a large pumpkin, oblong and purple, with razor-blade teeth, bulging black eyes . . .

Oh, no! Had the beast followed me?

The idea was too much. The whole night had been one scare after another. I wobbled dizzily, shivering with cold. Inside my soaked sneakers my toes were numb. My head ached. My stomach felt as if I'd been punched when I wasn't looking. I tried shaking the cobwebs out of my head, blinked a couple of times, and gingerly touched my forehead. Ouch! A crab apple–sized welt sent shooting pains out both my ears.

Poor Silver. Trapped inside that awful house, captured by ... ghouls. Had they already boiled him in their steaming kettle? Had he somehow managed to escape? Why hadn't he answered me when I called? What should I do now? Head for home, the police, the neighbors? Head for the hideaway as Silver had said? No, there was no time to lose. He was my best friend. I'd have to finish what we'd started. But how?

Sounds — middle-of-the-woods, nighttime sounds — surrounded me. The gurgle of the stream I'd splashed across, the hoot of an owl, the steady noise of some kind of insects, a sinister sound, like a man snoring — some animal.

I looked around, found a heavy limb the size of a baseball bat, and reluctantly headed back toward the abandoned house. Getting in would be no problem. I'd climb the tall bush next to the pantry window. But once inside, would I have the courage to face what had to be faced?

I was across the stream before I realized just how big a fool I was. Silver hadn't been captured by ghouls, he was the ghoul, the beast in the corner. Hunched down behind a candle that he'd lit himself, a purple-colored pumpkin for a head (no wonder his knapsack was so bulgy!), ignoring my shouts, waiting for me to come looking for him, to poke my head around the corner, then snarling like a mad dog, scaring me half to death. It'd been Silver all right, no doubt about it.

The mystery was over and with it my flight.

"Damn you, Silver!" I shouted. "You just wait!"

I hurried now, straight for the house. Imagine him playing a trick like that on his best friend. What had gotten into him?

"Silver!" I shouted.

Again, he didn't answer.

"Silver! It's me, Tramp. You may as well come out. I know what you're up to and it won't work anymore."

I was standing in the middle of what must've been the living room, the baseball bat–limb resting on my shoulder, not ten feet from where Silver had tricked me. But now the room was empty. No pumpkin, no knapsack, no candle, no Silver.

"Silver!" I shouted. "If you don't come out now, I'm leaving." And that's exactly what I would've done had a noise not stopped me, a noise like the moan of the wind in the chimney flue — only it wasn't.

"Trrrrrrrraaaaammmmp."

Was I scared? No. Given the circumstances, on any other night my hair would've probably stood up and touched the ceiling, but not tonight. Silver had already played enough tricks on me and no noise coming from the basement, no matter how eerie sounding, was apt to frighten me again. Not tonight.

"Trrrrrrrraaaaammmp."

Even without a flashlight, it wasn't a problem finding the basement door. The light from the moon came in through the cracks along the sides of the shades and helped light my way. I found the door in the kitchen, sandwiched between some cabinets and an old iron stove. I turned the handle and the basement door swung silently open.

"TRRRRRRRRAAAAAMMMP."

"Silver, cut it out."

"Crossed thumbs, see the dead run," he said in a whisper. "Down here."

I began to descend the steep stone stairs. The footing was slippery. To support myself, I reached a hand out and touched the stone wall to one side of me. It's coldness sent a shiver through my body. At the foot of the stairway, I stopped. The basement, save for a single beam of light at the far end, was as dark as could be.

"Silver!"

"Shush," he whispered. "Over here."

I was in no mood for games. "Why did you do that to me?" I said.

"Never mind that now," he said. "Look."

His flashlight shone on a small door.

"Here's where they hide the coffins," he said.

"There are no coffins," I said. "No coffins, no ghouls, nothing."

"Well, then explain this," he said. "I've been all over this house, and this is the only place I can't get inside. The door's locked. The only door that's locked in the entire house. The question is why."

"Could be anything," I said. "Could be —"

"Hey-o!" he shouted, startling me so bad that I dropped the tree limb I'd been holding all this time. It bounced once and rolled a little way across the floor.

He was pointing his flashlight at the base of the door. There was a space about three inches wide, between the base and the floor. All at once he dropped to his knees, put his face to the floor, and directed the flashlight beam inside .

"There's . . . there's . . . OH, NO!" he screamed, leaping to his feet. "It's an eye! A face with one eye! Run, Tramp! Run for your life!"

We were two blurs in the dark. Across the basement and up the stairs, through the kitchen and — "Throw open the bolt!" — out the front door, running even faster than I'd run before. There was nothing to stop us now. Nothing, that is, until a pair of steely hands closed around my throat, and I felt myself being dragged back, back toward the abandoned house.

7
Counting to Ten

I NEVER GOT THERE. PROBABLY BECAUSE I HAD MY eyes shut tight the whole time and was kicking and screaming so loud, I was the last to know what was happening. In between screams, I managed to hear Silver's familiar, though somewhat garbled, voice sputtering, "Let me up, will you? Come on, let me up."

Was he talking to the ghouls?

I stopped struggling and opened my eyes. The grip around my throat relaxed a bit, I got a look behind me, good enough to see the stern face of James J. O'Roarke, Chief of Police. A few yards away, a tag team of officers had wrestled Silver to the ground, where one held on to his ankles, another his arms, while a third sat heavily on top of his chest.

"Let me up, will you?"

I was never so happy to see the police in all my life.

The police, as you might expect, were not nearly so happy to see us.

"Okay, men, let him up," commanded the chief. "But be sure you've got a good hold. We wouldn't want either of these young fellas to get away, would we?"

The three police officers hauled Silver to his feet, then proceeded to march the two of us across the overgrown yard, down the driveway, and through the rusty iron gate — now open — to where two police cars waited, their blue and red spotlights blinking on and off in the dark.

Now that I wasn't so scared anymore, I began to feel embarrassed by the trouble Silver and I had caused. A small group of neighborhood people had gathered under the street light, most of them in pajamas and bathrobes. I was glad when I didn't recognize any of them, especially the old wart who kept hollering, "Lock 'em up! Lock 'em up and throw away the key!"

I knew one person who'd recognize me, though, as

soon as he got a good enough look in the light of the police car — Chief O'Roarke. To make matters worse, he was friends with my dad. They even went on fishing trips together. He knew Silver, too, but for other reasons — some of the trouble Silver'd gotten into over the years.

"Well, well, what have we here?" the chief said, once he'd climbed into the front seat and had turned around to look at us. "If it isn't Tramp Steamer. And who's that with you, Tramp? Why, it's the Branch kid. Steven Branch, isn't it?"

"Please refer to me as Silver," said Silver.

Chief O'Roarke's face turned a shade or two darker. He took off his cap and wiped his brow. His pudgy face looked tired. I could tell, when he didn't say anything right away, that he was probably counting to ten, like my dad always did when he was trying to control his temper. I took the opportunity to warn Silver to keep quiet by giving him a hard kick in the ankle. When the chief spoke, his voice was calm, but it had lost all its natural good humor.

"Mr. Branch," he said sternly. "You and Mr. Steamer here have got yourselves a load of trouble. In one night, with your screams and flashing lights and fooling around, you've managed to disturb, and I might add, frighten, an entire neighborhood of peaceful people, trespass on private grounds, illegally enter a private dwelling, destroy property . . ."

"We didn't destroy anything, Chief O'Roarke," I said meekly.

"How about the window you broke?"

"We didn't break it. We found it like that."

"You did, did you? Tell me, what made you two boys go inside that house, anyway? I know it's Halloween, but what'd you expect to find in there?"

"Ghouls," I said.

"What?" said the chief, leaning over the seat as if he hadn't heard. Now it was Silver's turn to kick me under the seat.

"Gh — nothing," I said. "Can we go home now, Chief? We won't go inside there ever again. We won't go near the place, will we, Silver? Promise. It was a stupid thing to do. Stupid. We won't go anywhere near it again. Ever."

"I hope not," said the chief, starting up the engine. "And, yes, you can go home. In fact, I'll take you there myself. Steven, too. I'd very much like to have a talk with both your fathers."

My father! For the second time that night I'd see another adult counting to ten.

8
A Book of Spiders

MY MOM AND DAD WERE NOT PLEASED. MY ARRIVING home past midnight on a stormy Halloween night, filthy, scratched, bruised, my clothes in shreds, a welt the size of a crab apple sticking out on my forehead where I'd hit it on the ground, an exhausted mess standing at the front door, and with the chief of police, no less. Oh, sure, they were relieved to see me home and virtually all in one piece, but pleased? Not on your life.

Chief O'Roarke gave them a brief account of the gory details, the ones he knew. He mentioned, no doubt for my benefit, the dangers of old houses that had been vacant for some time, such as rotten floorboards, rats and bats, and that old houses were often havens for tramps and crooks, people on the run (he didn't mention ghouls). He also mentioned that I'd not been alone in my exploits, that Silver'd been with me, and that the two of us would have to share in the payment of a broken window. Any other punishment, he said to my parents, would be left up to them. After he left, I received the usual admonishments — actually, worse than usual — sent upstairs to take a shower, patched up (my mom doing the handiwork), and sent to bed with an ice pack for my forehead, spared further embarrassment until morning.

The outcome was that in addition to the chores I already had, like emptying wastepaper baskets, taking out the garbage, and making sure my room was clean, I now had to rake leaves every other day (when I didn't have basketball practice), wash the family car when necessary, and for the next two weekends, help my dad put up storm windows — four full days of work! My parents knew enough not to try to keep me away from The Silver Bullet. After all, he was my best friend and neighbor. Besides, I wouldn't be seeing him for a month, anyway. The day after Halloween I called his house and was told by his father that Silver had already gone to visit his mother at her apartment in New York City for the weekend, and from there would return to boarding school. He wouldn't be back home until the end of November. One more thing. My parents told me that the way I conducted myself for the next month would determine whether or not I'd be going to the junior high school Thanksgiving dance.

"Try to use better judgment in the future." That was my Dad's final remark, and the matter of Halloween night was closed. For him, that is, not for me.

What had Silver seen that made him scream like that and run for his life? I could think of four possibilities. That whatever he saw was only something that looked like an eye, maybe one of those cat's-eye marbles. Or that he'd seen the reflection of his own eye in a mirror (wouldn't the joke be on him?). Or that there really was someone or something — even an animal — hiding behind the door, dead or alive. Or, finally, like so much of what he'd done to me that night, that he'd made it all up — the eye, the screams, the running about, just to frighten me further. He seemed capable of doing anything.

Since I couldn't see Silver until Thanksgiving vacation, I thought of writing to him or calling him at his school, to demand an explanation. I did neither. A month was a long time for a mystery to remain unsolved, not to know for sure, but when we got around to talking about it I wanted to be looking at Silver face to face. That way I'd be certain if he was lying to me, playing games. With all the chores I had to do around home, plus schoolwork, basketball practice, and the new girl in class I had my eye on, the month passed quickly.

I found The Silver Bullet sprawled on the couch in his room, sipping a cream soda and reading a book, a weighty volume, the kind you might find in your grandmother's attic — a book about spiders. A ferocious looking, hairy-headed one was pictured on the cover beneath the word *Lycosa!*

"Tramp," he said, "did you know that the bite of a wolf spider has been known to cause madness in people? That it mesmerizes its victims before it kills them?"

"Forget spiders," I said. "What about that locked door in the basement? You didn't really see a face with one eye, did you?"

It was as if he, too, had been waiting all month for me to ask. Snapping the spider book shut, he bolted from the couch, took hold of my shoulders, and stared into my face.

"Tramp," he said, his voice filled with alarm. "Listen to me. I've never lied to you, you know that. Sure, I stretch the truth now and then, play some tricks I'm usually sorry for — that purple pumpkin head, ghouls and all, Halloween nonsense — but never an outright lie, not to you. I'm only saying this now because I want to be absolutely sure you believe me when I tell you I did see an eye staring back at me from under that door."

"Then I've got it all figured out," I said. "Simple. Behind the door was a mirror. What you saw under the door was yourself."

Silver dropped his hands from my shoulders. For a moment his dark eyes narrowed beneath his bushy eyebrows and a trace of anger flitted across his face.

"You know I wouldn't make a foolish mistake like that, don't you, Tramp? After all, I know what my own eye looks like."

"It was dark," I said.

"I had a flashlight," he said. "Remember?"

I did remember, and Silver had a point. It wouldn't have been like him to make such a silly mistake.

"If not a mirror, then what?" I asked.

"What else?" he said.

"You mean a real live person?"

"Alive as you and me," he said. "Unless dead people blink."

"But Chief O'Roarke . . ."

"Yeah," said Silver. "He told my father the one about tramps and convicts, too."

"You don't believe him?"

"I believe him," said Silver. "Only the eye I was looking at was a woman's. I'm pretty sure."

I thought about this for a moment, a new development.

"I wonder what she was doing," I said.

"Hiding," he said, "from us. She probably made those noises we heard."

"But why was she there in the first place?"

"Who knows?" said Silver. "Maybe someday we'll find out. But I think we'd better lie low for a while. Stay away from the place. My father's threatening to pull me out of school, send me someplace even farther away, if I don't stay out of trouble."

"Don't worry," I said. "I'm not about to go sneaking inside any more empty houses. Not yet, and not without you."

"Good," he said. "Then take a look at this."

He took up his knapsack, rummaged around inside, and pulled out a flat metal box the size of a *Reader's Digest*. He snapped open the lid and held the box out for me to see. Inside, eight legs pointing out, was the brown remains of the largest spider, dead or alive, that I'd ever seen.

The sight of it made me jump. "Where'd you get it?" I exclaimed.

"Found it," he said. "Curled around the outside doorknob to my bedroom."

"You're kidding? How? Why?"

"Don't know," he said, shaking his head. "But I do know one thing. We've got another mystery brewing, for real."

9
Sally West

ONCE AGAIN, SILVER WAS RIGHT — WE DID HAVE another mystery brewing, one that turned out to be stranger and more terrible than the eye under the door. Where would anybody get a spider big enough to curl around a doorknob? And why the doorknob to Silver's bedroom? Was it a sign, a warning, an omen? Was it somehow connected to our Halloween adventure? Something told me that it was.

To solve a mystery — a good one — takes some time. This was especially true for Silver and me. After all, he was only home from boarding school on vacations, which tended to leave some pretty cold trails for us to follow. Then again, solving mysteries sometimes takes being in the right place at the right time. This was exactly the case with the dead spiders — and the mysterious eye. Almost two whole months would go by before, unexpectedly, the key to the mysteries would land in our laps. Lastly, there were plenty of other things to keep us busy. For me it was homework (math, science, English, you name it), basketball, and . . . girls. Or should I say girl? A warm, sweet-voiced, silky-smooth girl named Sally. Sally West. During the summer, Sally and her family — her mom was an artist — moved into an old stone house downtown, next door to the fire station. Sally and I were in the same grade at school, but except for math we had different teachers, and practically the only times I ever saw her were at lunch, in the halls between classes, and before and after school.

Usually when a new kid begins school, it's tough for him or her to make friends. I guess it's only natural, though I wouldn't know myself, having lived in the same town and known the same kids all my life. Sally, however, was different. In a little more than two months, since school began in September, she had become, without a doubt, one of the most popular girls in the seventh grade.

There were good reasons for this. From what I could gather, she was smart, but not too smart — maybe she kept it to herself; pretty, but not too pretty; friendly, but not pushy or sticky-sweet like some kids are. She was cheerful and kind, and when she spoke it was in a soft, musical voice — the sound of a flute — that made others want to listen to her.

She was certainly nice to look at, which I did, inconspicuously, every chance I got. She was small and sleek as a bobcat, though a little more mature than most seventh-grade girls, if you know what I mean. Sometimes she wore wildly colorful dresses, other times shirts and blue jeans, and when she walked, she sort of swayed like the branches of a birch tree, gliding along, never seeming to be in a hurry, no matter what. She had a pretty, almost perfectly round face, tan skin, and a tiny dot of a nose and mouth. I'd never gotten close enough to see the color of her eyes, but I imagined them to be the same as her hair — charcoal black, which she wore long and straight, almost to her waist, and I liked it whether she wore it loose or in a single braid. She could've been part Indian for all I knew, and when she smiled — never once at me — I'd get a queasy feeling in my stomach, the kind I got from bouncing up and down too long on the trampoline.

Sally, oh, Sally. I couldn't seem to get her off my mind. I thought about taking her to movies and parties and going over to her house with nothing special to do. I thought about the sassy way she talked to the older guys at school, about the clothes she wore, about the way she glided through the halls among her friends. Recently, I'd begun to think about her in ways I never had before, about sitting with her in the dark and all the things that'd happen that I'd heard other guys talk about, my older brother, Tommy, and his friends, for instance.

I kept her address and phone number on a piece of paper in my wallet, just in case I might need it. So far I hadn't. I kept making mental notes of out of the ordinary things that I'd noticed about her. The strange food she brought for lunches, sardine sandwiches and huge mushrooms stuffed with glop; the way she'd walk home from school in her bare feet, even on fairly cold and rainy days; the incredibly loud noise that her nose made when she blew it into her red kerchief; the science fiction books that she read, one after another — you didn't see too many girls doing that.

Of course, having her in school was pure torture. To give you an idea, one day about a month ago, I was on my way home from school after basketball practice, when who should I see sitting all by herself on the concrete steps in front of the school? Who else but Sally? Now you have to understand that in the few months Sally had been in town I'd never once spoken to her. Oh, I may have mumbled a "hi" now and then if I accidentally bumped into her in the hall, but that was it — not another word. And that isn't like me at all. I'm usually pretty talkative and not that shy either. But ever since September and the start of school, when I began to get these feelings about Sally, instead of making friends with her, I'd walk just as fast and as far as I could in the opposite direction. Hiding in the washroom, sneaking around the halls, poking my head inside my locker. Anything to avoid having to speak to her. Weird! It sure was to me.

Anyway, there was Sally, by herself on the steps in front of school, and there I was walking right by her. If she hadn't looked up from her book and seen me right away, I probably would've done a quick about-face, sneaked around back of the building, and taken another route home.

"Hi," she said, startling me.

It would've been impossible to ignore her, rude too. So, casual as a pirate about to step off a gangplank into the mouth of a hungry shark, I edged closer. All the time my mind was racing — what in the world was I going to say to her?

"Hi," she said again, and smiled.

It was the smile that got me, a pearly-white smile in the middle of all that black hair, that froze me on the spot. What must she have thought of me, all skin and bones, my turtlelike neck sticking straight up out of my jacket collar, my hair a brown weed, my legs and arms way too long, my feet as large and as flat as a couple of snowshoes. What must she have thought?

"Hi," I managed to say, but that was all. The special words I'd practiced to say to her at a time like this, when it was just the two of us, all came out backward and my voice began to sound as if my mouth were full of food. In the end I managed a few grunts, a few animal noises, something like "SNORBLE, GRRBLUT, TREEKLE," overly loud, and had run off like the coward I was, feeling all hot inside and ashamed for even trying, head down, heart pounding, my chance gone.

I stayed even farther away from Sally after that. Determined, I was extra careful not to cross paths with her, even accidentally, ever again. The hardest times were during math class, when I was forced to be in the same room with her. I was sure she was laughing at me behind my back. I also crossed out her address and phone number from the piece of paper in my wallet, but not so much that I still couldn't read the writing. And it wasn't until a few days before the junior high school Thanksgiving dance that I wrote Sally's address and phone number over again so I could read them more clearly.

Silver, it turned out, was wrong. He'd been telling me, "Bravery begins and ends by putting one's life on the line for one's friends," like those two Greek mythological characters, Damon and Pythias. For me, bravery began and ended by trying to mumble a few monosyllabic words to a girl, if that particular girl's name was Sally West.

10
A Muddy Situation

"YOU THINK YOU'LL ASK A GIRL TO DANCE TONIGHT?" said Silver.

The two of us, wearing winter coats and hats, were clumping along the icy street toward the junior high school, where, in a few minutes, the annual seventh to ninth grade Turkey Time Dance would begin. The snow had fallen steadily throughout the day, freakishly early for this time of year, and had finally showed signs of letting up, but the footing underneath was still slippery and the going slow.

I tried to ignore Silver's question, but he wouldn't let me.

"Well?" he said. "Are you or aren't you?"

"What?" I said.

"Going to ask a girl to dance."

"I might," I said, not about to let Silver or anyone else in on my intentions. "Are you?"

"Doubt it," he said. "Though there might be one or two good looking enough to take a chance on. Not that they'd come near some of the girls I know at Courtland."

"Oh, sure," I said sarcastically. "And what makes prep school girls so special?"

Silver chuckled, a bit nervously I noticed. In fact,

he'd been acting strange all day, jumping about in his room from one thing to another, laughing and talking a whole lot more than usual. He'd even combed his hair. "You're a little young yet, Tramp," he started to say in answer to my question, sounding like my older brother, Tommy. But I hit him with a snowball, shutting him up, and chased after him, slipping and sloshing down the street, hearing his ringing laugh all the way to the school.

In truth, I did have a definite plan for the dance. All day — all month — I'd given it careful consideration, step by step, how I'd get Sally to dance with me.

It wasn't going to be easy, that I knew. Not easy at all. But the thing was, I was feeling super, maybe confident was a better word, and not even Silver's teasing could dissuade me from thinking that good luck was about to come my way. Already the day had been one of the luckiest in my life. I had unexpectedly earned a pocketful of money shoveling snow for my dad and some of the neighbors, so I wouldn't go off to the dance completely broke. The ugly red splotches that had been cruising around on my face had all suddenly and magically moved to my forehead, where I could hide them with my hair. But best of all by far, Sally had actually waved to me from across the street in front of my house that morning. She must've been on her way to visit one of her friends. A wave — now that's something!

School dances were held in the gymnasium. When Silver and I got there, the entrance to the gym was crowded and noisy with kids taking off their coats and

hats and waiting for friends to arrive. I was glad when I
didn't see Sally. Before anything happened, I wanted to
find a place by myself in the darkened gym. Once there,
I could think about my plan and wait for the right time
to ask her to dance.

"Let's get something to eat," Silver suggested, once
we were both inside.

"Go ahead," I said. "I'll meet you later."

I found a seat on the corner of the stage, where I had
a clear view over the heads of the kids standing below
me on the gym floor. There were crowds of kids everywhere. Many of them, mostly older kids in the eighth
and ninth grades, were already dancing to some loud
music that was coming out of a jukebox in the far corner, beneath an enormous papier-mâché turkey that
hung suspended from the ceiling. Clumps of kids
crowded together in a ring around the outside of the
dance floor. Others sat by themselves or in small groups
on benches that were pushed up against the walls. On
other nights, I'd probably have been with some of the
guys, but not tonight. Tonight was different.

From my seat on the stage, I began to look for Sally.
I wanted to keep an eye on her while I rehearsed the
speech I'd made up, to make sure that it was clear in my
mind. Then I'd wait for just the right moment, when
she wasn't surrounded by all her friends, inconspicuously worm my way across the gym floor, sneak up
behind her, and — HERE I AM! — ask her to dance.

I gave the dance floor a good going over, and was
glad when I didn't see Sally dancing with some other

guy, especially an older one. The less competition the better. She wasn't dancing and she wasn't watching the dancers either. Where was she? I looked up and down the rows of kids sitting on benches along the walls. The dim lighting and all the papier-mâché decorations, balloons, and streamers crisscrossing the room made it hard to see the faces of the kids at the opposite end of the gym, but I was pretty sure Sally and her friends weren't among them.

"She's not here," I said out loud. "She's not here, and she isn't coming."

A sudden thought caused me to whirl around. Like myself, a few dozen other kids were sitting on the edge of the stage, none of them Sally. Whew!

I surveyed the gym one more time — the dance floor, the ring of watchers, the rows of benches. No Sally. With all my plans for the dance, it'd never occurred to me that she might not be coming. It made me feel sad that I wouldn't get the chance to know her better, yet somehow relieved, too. It's hard to explain, but for the first time that night I noticed how sweaty I was, right through my shirt, and felt the muscles in my back as tight as a couple of clenched fists.

"Hey, Tramp, over here!"

It was Silver. He'd spotted me from a group of guys he knew (he knew practically everyone in town) over by the refreshment stand.

All at once I began to feel better. It was still early, plenty of time to have fun with Silver and some of the guys, pitch some coins outside, get something to eat after the dance was over. So what if I didn't get to ask Sally to dance? There'd be other dances, and for the next one, I'd come up with an even better plan.

With that thought in mind, I bounded off the stage, turned, and tumbled headlong into — Sally West.

"Hey, watch out!" she said sharply, giving me a shove. "What're you trying to do, run me over?"

Run! a voice inside me shouted. Run!

I took a half-step toward the exit, when Sally's voice stopped me.

"I didn't know you came to dances, Obe."

"You didn't?" I sputtered, trying not to look at her. As much as anything, I was surprised that she knew my middle name — Obediah. Obe was my former nick-name.

A few of Sally's girlfriends giggled.

Say something, I told myself. Anything. But the words wouldn't come, not even my carefully prepared speech. It was as if my mind were a blank piece of paper folding itself up into a tiny square. Still, I somehow found the courage (where I'll never know) to look at her, straight into her pretty round face. A word formed on my lips, I took a deep breath, and managed to murmur "Dance?" in a soft, unfortunate voice, as a sick child might ask for a glass of water.

Almost at once, I regretted it. One after another, the girls on either side of Sally began to laugh, until a moment later they were all laughing together.

Run! the voice inside me shouted.

But I couldn't. My feet felt as if they were stuck in

mud up to the ankles, and they wouldn't budge an inch. Not one inch. All I could do was to stare helplessly at Sally's face, drowning under a wave of giggles.

"Sure," Sally said with a little hop. "Come on."

It *was* a lucky day.

11
The Hand-Me-Down Toboggan

FROM THAT TIME ON THINGS WERE DIFFERENT BE-tween Sally and me. Oh, not so much that anybody'd notice. I still more or less kept my distance, but I no longer went out of my way to avoid her, even talked to her a few times, usually on our way into and out of math class. And, without fail, every time I did, I couldn't help but think about dancing with her — five times in all! — and how easy and natural it seemed once my feet had become unstuck and she'd taken me by the hand and led me out onto the dance floor. There we joined about two hundred other kids, half a gym floor full, who were moving about, this way and that, fast or slow, whatever felt good, no matter what music was playing on the jukebox. Sally and I danced fast, about three feet apart, but as far as I was concerned that was close enough. Plenty close — at least for the time being. Five dances!

In the month that followed, whenever I talked to her, she was always friendly, asked personal (but not nosy) questions, and talked about ordinary things in an extraordinary way, a way that made you remember and think about what she said. It's hard to explain and I didn't really understand it myself until I got to know her better. At any rate, for the time being there was nothing to get excited about, because Sally talked that way to just about everyone. Even so, my mental list of unusual things about her continued to grow. Her eyes weren't black; they were two different colors — dark and darker — slightly out of focus, and not quite round.

About a month later, the day after Christmas, in fact, I met Silver in front of his house (he was spending part of Christmas vacation that year with his father) and together we walked in the direction of the town forest preserve, a wooded tract of conservation land that bordered the far end of our street. My mom and dad had given me a toboggan for Christmas, and I was anxious to try it out.

It wasn't a brand-new toboggan, not at all. It was instead a very special old one, one that had originally been bought by my grandfather, handed down to my dad when he was a boy, and now handed down to me. (Why not my brother Tommy? He hadn't wanted it; he hated outdoor winter sports.)

The toboggan was quite a construction. Seven feet long, made of dark wood, it had a sleek, unbreakable appearance. Three shiny silver handles were fastened to each side, along with a tug-rope to help you hold on while you sped down hills. At one time there'd been some fancy cushions to sit on, but they'd long been lost. "A true tobogganer doesn't need cushions," my dad said. On the curved front end, along with the marks of age (cracks and splinters) there was a hand-carved picture of a deer's head, complete with antlers.

It was a typical late December day. The most recent storm had added a thick layer of snow to the already ice-crusted ground. The temperature was on the rise from zero. The warming southern winds had blown away the last of the ominous gray storm clouds. As Silver's and my boots crunched and squeaked down the icy road, a glassy sun shone in our faces.

Everywhere there were people about, shovelers and ice-choppers, whistling and wisecracking, yelling back and forth to one another over the tops of snowdrifts sandwiched between driveways. More than a few people were showing off new snowblowers that spouted columns of fine white snow. There were snowball throwers and snowmen makers, sledders and skaters and cross-country skiers, even a jogger or two, puffing alongside the road, beneath heavy sweatsuits, gloves, and stocking caps.

Across the highway, at the edge of the forest preserve, the ground rose up a steep incline, where it joined a line of trees. In the summertime the foliage formed a natural wall, an obstacle that deterred most people from pushing their way through and beyond. But not Silver and me. Summer or winter, we simply dug in, scaled the incline, slipped between the branches, and acre upon acre of hilly, wooded land was ours.

The only way to carry the toboggan was over our heads, as you would a canoe. It had no pull rope. Even so, it didn't take us long to reach our destination: a long, slowly winding hill, as good a place as any to practice using the toboggan and not have to worry about going too fast and losing control.

"You sit up front," I told Silver, who was quieter than usual that morning. He'd mistakenly left his knapsack at boarding school, and would have to do without it for the entire Christmas vacation, at both his father's house and his mother's apartment in New York City, where he was bound that afternoon. Forgetting the knapsack was, to use his words, a "portent of doom." How I wish he hadn't been right.

The ride downhill was good, not great. The toboggan scooted over the frozen layer of snow, straight as a torpedo, never once tilting either right or left to make either of us have to steer. All we had to do was hang on, which wasn't difficult at all. We were only going about ten miles per hour. Part way down the hill a small rise caused the toboggan to fly up in midair and bang down on the other side. But except for the bump, the snow spraying our faces, and the good length of the ride, the experience was a disappointment. Silver felt the same.

"It's not fast enough," he said, after we'd each taken a turn in the front and back position. "I feel like an old lady out for a stroll."

"I've got it!" I said. "Let's do some stunts, acrobatics. Purposely make things harder than they are."

"You mean ride backward and stand up, stuff like that?"

"Yeah."

"Okay," he agreed, but with less enthusiasm than I'd hoped. "I'll think up a trick for you to do. Then you think up one for me. Then we'll do one together."

"Sounds good," I said.

And for the next hour or so that's just what we did. We each went down the hill sitting backward so we couldn't see where we were going. We went down standing up, together at first, then one at a time, without holding on. We played King of the Toboggan, each of us trying to knock the other off while the toboggan slid its way down the hill. We played "target practice," and took turns pelting the toboggan rider with snowballs. Last of all we played "bail out," leaping from the toboggan at the exact moment it flew over the bump and was suspended in midair. After that last game our coats and hats were covered with snow, my gloves were wringing wet, and I could feel chunks of snow beginning to melt inside my boots.

"Let's try something new," Silver suggested.

"I'm all out of games," I said. "But we could play 'bail out' again. That was the best yet."

"We've already done that three times," said Silver. "I mean something new, like move to a new spot."

"Where?"

"Think, Tramp. You know these woods as well as I do."

I thought for a moment. "Well," I said, "there's the apple grove."

"Too many trees," Silver said.

"There's the other side of the pond."

"Yeah, that might be good, except I don't think it's

any steeper than here. But wait. If we walk to the far end, where we found that dilapidated car last summer, isn't there a hill around there somewhere?"

"There sure is," I said. "But it's too steep. And there's a stream at the bottom of it."

"Maybe," he said.

"You know there's a stream, Silver. We've fished in it."

"I mean 'maybe' about it being too steep. Of course there's a stream, but it'll be frozen over this time of year."

"Lots of trees, too," I said.

"You're probably right, but let's take a look anyway."

12
Dead Man's Shoot

IT TOOK US ABOUT FIFTEEN MINUTES TO REACH THE spot we'd talked about. Silver knew the way better than I did and tramped along in the ice and snow at a quick pace, forcing me to keep up with him, the toboggan above our heads. All the exercise we were getting had made me quite warm, except for my feet which were freezing cold inside my wet boots and socks.

One look at the hill near the dilapidated car (why somebody'd drive a car into the woods and leave it there was beyond me) made me bristle with alarm. It was steep, much steeper than I remembered. In fact, it dropped practically straight down at a ninety-degree angle. We were standing on the edge above it, holding the toboggan upright between us. From that vantage point, I got the same dizzy feeling I got the few times I'd climbed out of the third-story attic window onto my roof at home and looked out over the gutter to the ground below. That's a pretty good comparison because the hill we were standing above was just that high — as high as a three-story building.

I poked my head around the side of the toboggan and looked at Silver. He had a funny smirk on his face, as if he'd just swallowed a tablespoon of foul tasting medicine and discovered he'd taken the wrong kind. "Impossible," he was muttering under his breath. "Impossible." He didn't like it when he was licked.

I was quick to agree. "Right," I said. "There's no way we're going to ride my toboggan down that."

He pushed the hood of his parka back off his head. His mess of silver hair stuck out all over. "It's too risky," he said, trying to convince himself by talking out loud. "It's much too steep and narrow. And even though there aren't any trees to watch out for on the way down, we'd run into that big clump at the bottom before we'd have a chance to stop the thing."

"Yeah," I said. "And beyond the trees is the stream."

Silver grunted.

"Let's go," I said.

He ignored me. "Still," he said, "somebody did it."

"What?"

"Look at those tracks in the snow. Somebody went down this hill on a sled, more than once by the look of it."

I took a cautious look over the edge. Silver was right. On the side of the precipice were a dozen narrow sled tracks, beginning at the top from where we stood, dropping vertically down the side, twisting and winding their various ways among the trees at the bottom, maybe even reaching the stream.

"Somebody brave —" I began to say, when a loud voice — almost a growl — stopped me.

"Welcome to Dead Man's Shoot, boys!"

Startled, both Silver and I whirled around. Behind us, no more than ten feet away, stood five or six tough-looking older kids, holding onto a couple of six-foot sleds and a black Doberman pinscher on a chain leash. I didn't recognize any of them, and one, the largest one with the dog, I wouldn't have been able to recognize anyway. He was wearing a ski mask, black and red checkered, pulled down over his head and face, with two round openings for his eyes and an ice-crusted slit for his mouth. They must've been sledding, heard us coming, and hid in the bushes.

"Thinkin' of goin' down Dead Man's Shoot in a toboggan?" said Ski Mask, coming toward me.

"N-no," I started to say, when Silver cut me off.

"It's none of your damn business what we do," he said, sticking out his chest.

Ski Mask laughed, an ugly laugh that sounded as if his throat were full of spit. A couple of his friends laughed, too. The Doberman growled. Then, without warning, Ski Mask reached out a huge gloved fist and grabbed the top of my cap, yanking it down tightly over my eyes. "Hey!" I heard Silver shout, but it was too late. Ski Mask knocked me down in the snow and pushed the toboggan on top of me. It all happened so fast that I didn't have time to brace myself, cry out, or anything. I heard what sounded like a tremendous scuffle going on around me, but with my cap covering my eyes and my face pressed into the snow, I couldn't see a thing. I couldn't move either. Someone, probably Ski Mask, had jumped on top of the toboggan, squashing me, my breath coming out in a rush.

No sooner did I regain my breath than I was yanked to my feet, my cap still over my eyes. I took a wild swing, but hit nothing. A handful of snow was shoved into my mouth and I was pushed back down again, only this time on top of the toboggan, not beneath it. Behind me, Silver was swearing his head off. Then there was a dull whack, someone wheezing for air, and a body (it turned out to be Silver) slammed against my back. All at once the toboggan slid forward, the ground gave way. We'd been shoved over the side!

It was over in a matter of seconds. The toboggan thundered down the precipice, so steep for much of the chaotic ride that the toboggan left the ground and we were flying. Then — CRASH! — we landed at the bottom with an awful jolt, so powerful that my chin snapped forward between my knees and hit the toboggan's curved wooden frame with a loud crack. If only my mouth hadn't been open at that exact moment (I was spitting out snow), everything might've been all right. Instead, blood splattered everywhere. My teeth had come down on the tip of my tongue, slicing the tip in half.

Almost at once my mouth filled with warm blood, which ran out my nose and down my chin, smearing my coat, pants, boots, everything. A lightning bolt of pain shot through my face and head. Under my cap my eyes welled up with tears. Still, the toboggan sped on. Down the narrow, icy path, through the clump of trees, steering itself along the grooves the sleds had made, coming to rest on the bank of the frozen stream, where it hung precariously.

When it finally stopped, I scrambled to my feet, clutching my mouth in pain. I pushed my cap back above my eyes. Behind me someone was running (Silver, who'd been thrown free at the bottom of the hill), but I was too hurt and scared to move. Farther away there were the sounds of laughing, hoots and hollering, and a dog barking, a piercing sound that cut through all the other noise. I wobbled dizzily and fell back down. I let my head fall between my legs, afraid to spit out the blood that poured through the slice in my tongue.

Then Silver was beside me.

"Spit it out, Tramp!" he was shouting. "Spit out the blood so I can take a look."

I did (I was too weak not to), and a moment later looked down at a bright red puddle of blood which was slowly seeping into the snow between my legs.

"Open your mouth!" Silver commanded. When I did, the pain caused tears to pour down my cheeks.

Silver took hold of my chin and peered inside my mouth. He let out a low whistle. "What a mess," he said. "But you'll live. Come on, Tramp. I'll help you up. We've got to get you home and to a hospital. Your tongue's going to need some stitches."

I tried to ask him about the big kids, but it hurt too much to talk, the words came out garbled, and a new surge of blood poured out of the slice in my tongue.

"Don't talk," Silver said, giving me a handful of snow. "Talking will only make it worse. Hold this snowball to your tongue 'til we get home. I'm sorry I don't have my knapsack, I might've been able to do more. But for now the cold snow'll slow the bleeding. Don't swallow the blood, spit it out when you have to. Now let's get going."

I made a motion toward the toboggan. It had slid off the bank and onto the frozen stream.

"I can't carry it and help you," said Silver. "We've got to leave it here."

What followed was the most painful walk I ever took in my life. Even though we headed for the nearest road, it was slow going over the slippery snow, and we had to stop about ten times for me to spit out blood and replace the snowball to hold against my tongue. But when we did finally reach the road, the first driver who came along saw Silver wave and the bloody mess I was in, and stopped to lend a hand. He was a nice man who ended up driving us all the way to my house. You can imagine the expressions on my parents' faces when they saw me.

Silver waited with me while my dad got the car out of

the garage to take me to the hospital. He shook his head sadly. "It was all my fault, Tramp," he said. "If I hadn't been so wise with those jerks, none of this would've happened. But we'll get them back, don't worry. I know them, even the guy wearing the ski mask, him and his dog. We'll get them."

For the first time I noticed that Silver was bleeding, too — a small, sore-looking cut on his chin, and a swollen eye as well.

He didn't accompany my dad and me to the hospital but ran off shouting that he had something to do. I thought that he meant catch the train to his mother's. But about an hour later, when my dad and I returned home, there was the toboggan stuck upright in the snow by the back door.

13
An Invitation to Lunch

IT WAS A WHOLE MONTH BEFORE I SAW SILVER AGAIN, unexpectedly banging on my back door late one Friday afternoon.

"What're you doing home?" I asked him. "Vacation isn't until next week."

"They shut the school down early," he said. "Heat costs or something. How's the old tongue?"

"Fine. The stitches are out and everything. I'm back to eating like a normal human being."

"Speaking of eating," said Silver. "Look what I found in my mailbox."

He pulled a bright pink envelope out of his coat pocket, an envelope that smelled of strong perfume. I looked at it closely. Silver's name was printed on the front, but that was all. No address, no stamp, just his name.

"Hand delivered," he said.

"Some girl," I said, kidding him about the color and the perfume.

He wasn't amused. "In a way," he said ambiguously. "Open it."

I opened the envelope and took out its contents, a single card, also pink and smelling of perfume. Somebody'd written in tiny, neat handwriting:

To: Steven Branch, 208 Post Road, Elyria, N.Y.

An invitation to lunch on Saturday, February 5th, at 1:00 P.M.

From: Miss Ethel and Miss Madeline MacElvie,
217 Post Road, Elyria, N.Y.

Purpose: To discuss a business proposition.

Informal.   R.S.V.P.

"It's from the crazy ladies!" I exclaimed, referring to the two secretive old crows, "recluses" my dad called them, because you rarely saw them outside their house, which was almost directly across the street from Silver's.

"Right you are," said Silver.

"You going to go?"

"Sure. Wouldn't you?"

I shrugged. "Lunch with two old ladies. A business proposition. It sounds pretty strange. Why didn't they just call you on the phone?"

"How should I know? They're like you say — crazy."

"What's this 'informal' mean? And these letters R.S.V.P.?"

Silver looked me up and down and shook his head. "Tramp, your lack of the social graces never ceases to amaze me. 'Informal' means you don't have to wear a tie or good pants or anything special. R.S.V.P. are the initials from a French saying, meaning to please let them know if you're coming."

I slipped the card inside the envelope and handed it back.

"I was going to ask your mom what she thinks," he said.

"Good idea."

We found my mom kneeling on a stepladder in the kitchen. She was trying to fix the venetian blind that one of my brother's friends had inadvertently broken playing Frisbee inside the house. Little Ginger was sitting by herself at the kitchen table, humming a nursery rhyme — "four and twenty blackbirds" — her wooden box of trinkets that she collected spread out before her.

"Mom," I said, "Silver —"

"Why, hello, Silver," she said, a mumble. She turned part way around on the ladder. A couple of nails were sticking out of her mouth. Her glasses had slid down on the bridge of her nose. The handle of a hammer stuck out of the back pocket of her jeans.

"Mom," I began again, "Silver's got a problem."

"Be right with you, boys," she said. She took up the hammer and pounded a new nail into the wall. We waited until she'd finished, a minute or two. "There, that ought to do it, temporarily. I wish your brother and his friends would be more careful. Oh, well." She sighed and climbed down off the ladder. "Now what can I do for you?"

"Silver got this letter . . ."

"Letter," said my mom. "That reminds me. Excuse me, dear, but if I don't tell you now I might forget. You got some mail today. It's right there."

At the far end of the kitchen table, on top of a pile of mail, was a pink envelope.

Silver and I exchanged glances. It hadn't occurred to us that I'd get one, too.

"What is it, Tramp?" asked my mom, pulling up a chair.

"The same thing Silver got. Only the name on it's different — my name. Silver and I've been invited to lunch at the crazy ladies' house. A week from tomorrow."

I handed the card to my mom. A smile spread across her face. "Very lovely," she said. "And perfumed, too. Interested?"

"Sure we are," said Silver.

"It might mean some extra money," I replied. "A business proposition . . ."

"Yeah," said Silver. Then he frowned. "Only . . ."

"Only what?"

"Only I don't want to be the one to R.S.V.P."

"Me either," I said. The idea of calling two old crows on the telephone bothered me as much as Silver.

"I'd be glad to do it for you," my mom said. "If you're both positive you want to go. It'd mean spending part of a Saturday afternoon lunching with two fancy old ladies."

We both nodded.

"Very well," she said. "Keep your sister company while I make the call. And by the way, 'eccentric' is a nicer word than 'crazy.' "

When she'd gone, Silver and I pulled up a couple of chairs and sat down at the kitchen table. To make room for my elbows, I pushed some of Ginger's junk aside. Something caught Silver's eye.

"Hey-o!" he exclaimed. "What's this?" He reached across the table and picked up a small glass bottle that was filled with a clear liquid. Floating in the liquid was a perfectly preserved spider, a much smaller version of the one Silver had found on his doorknob.

"Give it back," Ginger said to Silver. "It's mine."

"I won't hurt it," Silver said. "I just want to look at it for a second."

"No," she said sternly. "Give it back."

Reluctantly, Silver handed it over. But he didn't take his eyes off it. "Where'd you get it, Gin?" he asked.

"Found it."

"Where?"

"I don't remember."

"Think, Ginger," I said. "It could be important."

Ginger touched the tip of her nose with one of her tiny fingers. She screwed up her face in thought. Finally, just as I was about to lose my patience, she said, "I think I found this one on my lunchbox. The time I left it at the bus stop. But maybe it was on the windowsill, outside."

"What windowsill?" I asked.

"Yours, Pole."

"Mine!" I shouted in alarm, only half-kidding. "I'm done for."

"Wait a minute," said Silver. "I don't get it, Gin. Are you saying you found more than one spider?"

"I just told you," said Ginger. "I found two. One on my lunchbox, one on the windowsill."

Silver looked puzzled. "Were they both inside these little bottles, floating in formaldehyde?"

"Yep."

"Can I see the other one?"

Ginger took her finger off her nose and shook her head slowly back and forth. "I gave it to my friend, Betsy," she said. "For good luck."

"Good luck!" I said with a laugh. "A dead spider."

"Don't scare her," said Silver. "She's only a little kid."

"I'm not scared," said Ginger. "I saw her put it there. At night. I saw her out the window."

"Who?" Silver and I said at the same time.

"Miss Maddie," Ginger said. "Who you were just talking about."

"Mad Maddie, the crazy lady?"

I looked at Silver and he looked back at me, astonished.

"She's not crazy," said Ginger. "Her house is."

"Her house — ?" I started to ask, but Silver interrupted me. "How do you know?" he said.

"Me and Betsy been in it. They've got rocks that turn into candy when you eat them. And a moving wall and a hot room and a spider collection you can never see at the same time. And Mr. Bimbo, who talks, and when you turn on the faucets it comes out soda pop. And a plant that eats spaghetti."

I was too flabbergasted to speak. So was Silver. We both sat there, staring at Ginger, our mouths hanging open.

When we were younger, two or three years ago, we used to talk about sneaking inside the crazy ladies' house. Only we never did, not once, probably because one of them, Mad Maddie, almost never left the house (or so we thought), not even to walk around the yard, or poke her head out the door to get the newspaper. In fact, the only time we ever saw her leave the house was in broad daylight, when she and her sister, Ethel, also crazy we figured, went off to church in their car two or three times a year. A few times Silver and I had peeked inside the windows of their house at night, only to see a virtual forest of plants and greenery. And one summer we spent a whole week in one of Silver's second-story windows, spying on the crazy ladies' yard with binoculars, but saw nothing unusual, no mysterious goings-on, nothing. It'd all been a waste of time and we'd lost interest. But now . . . it seemed we should've gone up and knocked on the door and been invited in, as Ginger and her friend, two six-year-olds, must've done.

Anyway, it looked like we were about to get our chance.

"When did you see her do it, Gin?" Silver asked.

"What?"

"Leave the spider on Tramp's windowsill."

"I don't remember. It was dark. Miss Maddie's my friend. She winked at me."

Silver looked at Ginger and then looked back at me. Shoving his head down inside his coat, he twisted his face out of shape and bugged out his eyes in a mock look of horror, which made Ginger laugh. He mouthed the words "Mad Maddie" so that I could see them, then said out loud, "Now why do you suppose that old crow sneaks around in the dark, leaving dead spiders — wolf spiders, unless I'm wrong — all over the place?"

"Told you," said Ginger. "It's for good luck."

A few moments later my mom returned. It was all arranged. Lunch, a week from Saturday at one o'clock. My mom had a twinkle in her eye, but if she knew any more about it, she wasn't saying.

14
Spiders and Other Mysteries

ALL WEEK LONG SILVER AND I SPOKE OF ALMOST nothing but the mysteries surrounding the crazy ladies' house.

First, there was the matter of the "business proposition." No matter how many times I asked my mom about it, she retained her veil of secrecy. All she'd say was: "You'll find out soon enough." Thanks, Mom. Still, she was right. Silver and I *would* find out — on Saturday.

Then there were the mysterious aspects of the crazy ladies' house. Surely by "rocks changing into candy" Ginger meant rock candy. But what did she mean about the moving wall? The hot room (all I could think of was a sauna)? The spaghetti-eating plant? Who or what was "Mr. Bimbo, who talks"? Did soda pop really pour out of the faucets? Of course not. Then again, it wasn't like Ginger to lie.

Finally, there was the business of Mad Maddie and the spiders. The enormous one that Silver discovered on his doorknob, back in November, and the two Ginger found, one on my own windowsill. Why, if Ginger had actually seen her, was Mad Maddie sneaking about in the middle of the night delivering her strange presents? Silver kept reminding me that the bite of a wolf spider was known to cause madness in people. What did madness have to do with the good luck that Ginger spoke of? It all gave me the creeps.

Ginger had mentioned spiders in another way, too, the "spider collection you could never see at the same time," something like that. I asked her what she meant. She said: "Clam, clam, oyster shell, what I know I'll never tell."

It seemed that she and her friend Betsy had sworn each other to secrecy, and nothing I could say or do would make her give in. Six-year-olds. I was ready to flatten her.

Saturday — finally! At five minutes before one in the afternoon, I met Silver in front of his house and together we headed across the street. I was carrying under my arm a loaf of homemade bread that my mom had given me to take as a present to the two old crows. Beneath our winter coats, each of us was wearing his Sunday best — clean white shirt, tie, creased pants (the kind you have to take to the cleaners if they get dirty), and a pair of polished shoes. Even though the invitation said "informal," we both thought that it'd be wise to make, in my father's words, "a presentable appearance." After all, we were about to discuss a job, weren't we? And who'd hire anybody who looked like a bum?

To that end, I'd even gotten a haircut for the occasion, but Silver had merely drowned his mop of hair in some kind of greasy hair cream and squashed it flat on his head, probably using his hands. A few loose strands had escaped and were sticking out at right angles to his head, above his ears.

Surrounding the crazy ladies' house was a row of tall, dense bushes that even in winter hid the house from view of anyone passing by on the street. This in itself was pretty strange, considering that all the other houses in the neighborhood had normal front yards and shrubbery, but when I asked my mom about it, she just shrugged and said, "I guess the ladies don't want to be unnecessarily disturbed."

Once Silver and I set foot inside the front gate (hard to find if you didn't know where to look) and slipped between the tangle of bushes, nothing my mom or anyone else said could've convinced me that there was nothing unusual about the crazy ladies' house. It was like entering another world, an Alice-in-Wonderland fairy tale, where just about everything you expected to see you didn't and everything you didn't you did. Everything — colors, shapes, sounds — seemed weird.

Take the house. On first glance it appeared to be an ordinary house, just the sort of place where you'd expect two old ladies to live. Set among a thicket of leathery old oak trees at the bottom of a gully, the house was as clean and as neat and as white as a brand-new baseball — as if it had just been painted. Only, who paints houses in the wintertime? Another thing was that it had not one but two front doors, each about twelve feet high, large enough to accommodate a family of giants. And even though the house stood two stories tall, not a single window faced the street, except for one huge one on the second floor, which for some reason was all boarded up. Above the window, attached to the gutters all along the snow-covered roof, hung a row of icicles, like dinosaurs' teeth. On top of the roof was a small, round bell tower, missing the bell, and on top of that a rooster weathervane that was spinning around like a top.

Weird! Well, of course, it was a barn, a converted barn, I finally realized, with its double front doors and boarded up window, its bell tower and weathervane. But why hadn't I noticed this before, when I was younger and Silver and I were sneaking outside the house at night or spying from across the street with his binoculars? I probably had, only I was too young at the time to remember, and nighttime makes things look different, in this case better. And also it's a lot safer looking at something disturbing from the safety of your friend's house than standing right in front of it, about to go inside.

A winding, snow-shoveled path led from the front gate, down a steep, uneven row of steps, to one of the gigantic doors. Silver led the way, knapsack in hand, with me close behind. Following along, I noticed two things at the same time. One was the sound of birds, which kept getting louder and louder, dozens, maybe hundreds of birds, chirping, peeping, hooting, cawing, whistling, shrieking for all they were worth, many of them feeding at the dozens of what looked like hand-made bird feeders.

"I thought birds traveled south for the winter," I said out loud.

"Some do, some don't," said Silver, without turning

around. "What I don't get is why we never hear them on the street." Good question.

The other thing I noticed (it was hard not to) were the birdbaths, eleven of them at last count, in the front yard alone, each one piled high with a mound of snow. The snow made them look like ridiculously large mushrooms.

The tall bushes, the half-hidden gate, the spotlessly clean barn — er, house — the spinning weathervane, the steep path downward, the noisy birds and mushroom-birdbaths, all contributed to the overpowering feeling that I was about to experience something even more terrifying than the shock or two I'd gotten on Halloween.

At the front door this feeling went into high gear. I'd been so lost in my own thoughts that I never even bothered to ask Silver if he felt the same foreboding. I was about to when he pointed above our heads, at a black iron door knocker, made in the shape of a crow's head.

"Birds, birds, birds," he said, reaching up and giving it a couple of raps. "What a place!"

We listened as the sound of the knocking reverberated inside the house. Somewhere a bird screamed; far off there was the rumble of a deep voice. A door slammed, a bell jingled. There was the faint sound of a footstep. A minute went by, then two. The gigantic door remained closed. "Let's get —" I started to say, when Silver caught my arm. All at once, like the crack of a starter's pistol, the door burst open in our faces.

15
A Business Proposition

"HEY-O!" SILVER SHOUTED AS THE LOAF OF BREAD I'D been holding flew out of my hands like a football, bounced twice, and came to rest at the foot of the tiniest old lady I'd ever seen.

"My goodness, Stearns," said Ethel MacElvie in a voice that matched her body. "Is that any way to deliver a present from your mother? I take it the bread is from your mother, or did you bake it yourself?"

Silver had a good laugh at this suggestion.

"N-no, ma'am," I stammered, lurching forward to retrieve the bread. But Ethel beat me to it. For an old lady — in her seventies my mom had said — she could move like a cat.

She couldn't have been more than four and a half feet tall. A faded pink flowery dress covered her bony, miniature body, and on her feet were a pair of black old-fashioned shoes. For somebody that old, she had a pretty face, bright blue eyes, and a wrinkly nose. Her hair was pulled back in a tight little bun. Dangling from one ear, Gypsy-style, was a bell-shaped earring that jingled softly whenever she moved.

"Well, don't just stand there in the cold, boys," she

said. "Come on in before all my babies curl up and die of frostbite. Come on."

"Babies?" I said under my breath, once the door had closed behind us.

She heard me. "Forgive an old lady, Stearns," she said. "I call my plants 'babies.' It's a silly habit of mine, but old habits do die hard."

A quick look around showed why Silver and I had never been able to see inside the house. Practically every inch of available space was taken up by some sort of plant. Ivy clung to the lamps, bushy greenery hung upside down from flowerpots suspended from the ceiling, was sandwiched together on the windowsills, grew upward from dirt-filled planters at our feet. There was even a ten-foot-tall coconut tree growing out of a terrarium. The place had the soily smell and feel of a greenhouse, hot and cluttered and full of life. If you listened hard enough, you could almost hear movements in the dirt — the plants were growing.

"You sure do like plants," said Silver, an amazed look on his face.

"Yes, I do," said Ethel. She took our coats and hung them on hangers in a closet.

"Birds, too," said Silver.

"Why of course I do," said Ethel. "Though that's mostly Miss Maddie's hobby. Birds and — "

"Spiders," said Silver.

But Ethel missed Silver's remark, for at that exact moment she began coughing and for nearly a minute couldn't stop, a hoarse cough that sounded like that of a bad cigarette smoker. Four or five times during what turned out to be a short visit she had to stop what she was doing or saying and cough, long and hard, until I thought she was about ready to die.

"Now, boys," she said, after taking a moment to recover. "Please make yourselves at home. I won't be a minute in the kitchen and Miss Maddie will be down shortly ... I hope. I moved some of the plants off the divan," she said and pointed to the sofa, "so sit there if you like, or just poke around a bit while I'm gone."

And with that she was off to the kitchen, quick as could be, the tiny bell earring jingling at her ear.

"Perfect," said Silver. "Let's take a look around."

"Did you ever see an old lady move so fast?" I said.

"Or cough so bad?" said Silver. "Or wear so many rings? One on every finger."

I hadn't noticed.

"I can't believe all these plants," said Silver. "Look at this one coming out from under the rug."

"And this one," I said, gently tapping the pleasing bright yellow leaves of the one nearest me on the arm of the sofa. As soon as I had done so, the leaves snapped shut like the jaws of a turtle. "Did you see that!"

"The spaghetti-eater!" said Silver excitedly, his eyes open wide. He put his knapsack on the floor, dug his hand inside one of the pockets and pulled out a fistful of shiny cooked spaghetti. He'd come prepared for anything.

"Stand back!" he commanded. "And watch closely."

He removed a single noodle from the blob and dangled it directly above the plant, which by this time had again spread its leaves.

"Watch your fingers!" I cautioned.

But the plant didn't budge, no matter what Silver did, not even when he dropped the noodle between the open leaves. We watched it lying motionless, like a dead white worm.

"Drop in another one," I suggested, when suddenly there was the jingle of a bell. Ethel was returning.

"The spaghetti!" I whispered frantically. "Quick, into the plant!"

Just in time. The moment Silver dropped it in, Ethel darted around the corner.

"Do sit down, boys," she said, "while we wait for my tardy sister to honor us with her presence."

Silver and I obediently sat down on the sofa, me next to the plant, which was undoubtedly choking to death on the fist-sized blob of spaghetti. What if Ethel or, worse, Mad Maddie should see it? How embarrassing!

"Where is Mad — Miss Maddie?" I asked self-consciously.

Ethel pulled up a rocking chair and sat down. Silver was right. She did have rings on every finger. "Upstairs," she said. "She's looking for something she lost."

"Can we talk about the business proposition?" Silver asked, getting to the point. Was it my imagination or, mysteries or not, was he just as anxious to get out of there as I?

"BONG!" As Ethel was about to answer, a noise exploded on the first floor landing. Silver and I bounced up and down like a couple of rubber balls. Ethel seemed to hardly notice. But the "BONG!" was nothing compared to what we heard ten seconds later. A whirr, a click, an inhuman, metallic voice, like a robot shouting from inside a cave, which said, "The time . . . is . . . one . . . one . . . one . . . o'clunk," the last word falling off into a weak croak.

"Oh, I do have to have him checked, don't I?" said Ethel, mostly to herself. "He's been such a bad boy lately. Can't even tell time."

"Who?" asked Silver, as puzzled as I.

"Mr. Bimbo," said Ethel. "Our grandfather clock."

Silver flashed me a smile. One mystery had been cleared up, but a clock that talks?

"The business proposition?" said Silver.

"Yes," said Ethel. "Only I do wish Miss Maddie were here to help me. After all, it's half her idea. But I dare say, you both have been waiting long enough. So let me begin, and when I'm finished, tell me what you think."

Ethel made short work of it. Except for her tiny voice, she had a way of speaking that reminded me of trying to start my father's power lawnmower. She'd burst into high gear, speed along, sputter, come to a stop, sit silently for a moment, burst again into high gear, speed along, sputter, stop, and so on. After about eight or ten of these revolutions she was done. She and her sister wanted Silver and me to be gardeners. After the snow melted, the ground thawed, and the warmth of spring came, they wanted us to do their outside planting for them, a large vegetable and flower garden on the sunny south side of the house. Once we'd done the initial planting, they figured it'd take us no more than two or three hours each week to keep the garden in working order. Ethel and Mad Maddie would see to the rest.

"But why don't you do all of it yourself?" I asked and got a disgusted look from Silver.

"Young Stearns," said Ethel with affection. "We old people can only do so much. I haven't been feeling especially well, and you see what we've got going inside the house, the plants, the hot room, and all . . ."

"The hot room!" Silver and I both shouted at once.

"A greenhouse," said Ethel with a laugh that turned into a cough. We waited respectfully for her to finish, me fidgeting nervously. When she had, she said, "Don't tell me your sweet little sister and her friend never told you about our greenhouse?"

"Well, sort of," I said.

"Never mind. You shall see it soon enough. Directly after lunch, I expect. Now, where is that sister of mine? Maddie!"

She got quickly to her feet and darted across the room to the bottom of the stairs. "Maddie! You've been long enough. Lunch and two nice young men are waiting."

16
Lycosa!

A FACE APPEARED ON THE UPSTAIRS LANDING. A FACE
with large black raccoon's eyes that peeked suspiciously
around the corner at Silver and me, under the wide brim
of a straw hat.

"Come down, Maddie," Ethel implored. "There's
nothing to be afraid of." She held out her hands, palms
up, in Mad Maddie's direction. At the same time she
turned toward Silver and me and mouthed the word
"shy" under her breath, as if to explain.

Cautiously, one step at a time, Mad Maddie began to
descend the stairs, never once taking her eyes off us. I
could feel my stomach muscles tightening into a knot.

Mad Maddie was as tiny as her sister, and, for an old
crow, just as pretty. Only it was sort of hard to imagine — her being pretty. I got a good look though, because it must've taken Mad Maddie a full minute to
descend the stairs. She had on the same kind of flowery
dress as Ethel, the same black shoes, the rings on all her
fingers. A tiny chime earring jingled with each step that
she took. But for all the similarities, there was one big
difference. While Ethel, from her clothes to her pow-
dery make-up to the way she combed her hair, was me-
ticulously neat, Mad Maddie was a sloppy mess. Her
dress was awry, pushed too far back on her shoulders.

One of her shoelaces was untied. Her lipstick was splattered red all over her mouth. And beneath the brim of her Easter Sunday hat, her hair was flying out every which way. Still, despite all the confusion and untidiness, she was as pretty and frail as a hummingbird.

"What now?" said Silver under his breath.

When Mad Maddie reached the bottom of the stairs she took her sister's hand and, a smile brightening her face, let herself be led slowly forward, across the room to the sofa. Silver and I stood up.

"Steven, Stearns, I'd like to introduce my sister, Madeline MacElvie."

"Hi," Silver said. I mumbled the same. Usually when people are shy they drop their eyes or stare out into space when they meet someone for the first time. Not so with Mad Maddie; her eyes were riveted on Silver. I could feel him shift his weight from foot to foot, and noticed the sickly sweet smell of perfume, the same as on the invitations.

Ethel broke the spell. "Lunch is ready," she announced. "This way, please."

Silver and I followed the two old ladies into the next room. It, too, was covered from floor to ceiling with all sorts of vegetation. In the center of the room was a highly polished dining room table. On top of the table four place settings had been neatly arranged. Mad Maddie took a seat at the far end of the table, Silver and I on either side of her, facing each other. Ethel disappeared through the kitchen door.

An awkward silence followed. Mad Maddie sat smiling, never once taking her eyes off Silver. I could see by the look on his face that the tension was beginning to get to him. I flashed my squashed-bug face at him. He saw it, tried not to laugh, but the tension was too much. In a moment both of us were howling with laughter and kicking each other's shins under the table. Finally, Silver got control of himself, cleared his throat, turned toward Mad Maddie, who, beneath the brim of her hat, was beaming with joy, and was about to address her when —

"BONG!" Mr. Bimbo bellowed from the first floor landing. "The time . . . is . . . one . . . one . . . one . . . thirty." Again the robot voice ended in a croak. At the same time Ethel, full of conversation, burst through the kitchen door, carrying a steaming pot on a wooden serving board.

"Soup's on," she was saying, even before the kitchen door had swung to a close. "Hope you boys, excuse me, young men, enjoy good, homemade vegetable soup. Vegetables from our very own garden, naturally. Miss Maddie and I are vegetarians, you see. So I hope you won't mind the absence of meat this lunchtime. Of course, we do keep a bit of roundsteak on hand for one or two of the plants, so if you'd rather a hamburger . . ."

"No, thanks," said Silver. "The soup's fine." But as he was saying this, he was looking at me, probably to make sure that I'd heard correctly — meat for plants!

"Well, good," said Ethel. "Pass me your bowl, Steven. Stearns, be so kind as to pass me Miss Maddie's bowl as well as your own. Maddie, Stearns and Steven are considering our offer of employment. The final terms haven't been worked out yet, but I think two dollars an hour for each plus a share in the vegetables should be sufficient. Don't you?"

Mad Maddie nodded, her gaze continuing to rest uncomfortably on Silver.

"Doesn't she speak?" Silver asked.

"Oh, yes, dear. Maddie, do stop staring at Silver. It's most impolite. But she's quite shy around strangers. Always has been. And now, of course, she rarely sees them. You see, except for church she never leaves the house."

Silver gave me a look of alarm, his silver eyebrows arching high on his forehead. I didn't know whether to laugh or cry. Mostly, I was totally confused. If Mad Maddie wasn't the one leaving dead spiders all over the place, then who the heck was? And who'd winked at Ginger outside my bedroom window?

Silver wasn't about to be put off any longer. "Miss MacElvie," he began, addressing Ethel. "There are a number of things I'd like to clear up. For instance, do you have rocks that turn into candy?"

By this time Ethel had finished ladling and had passed back the bowls, brimming with delicious-smelling soup. Now she replaced the lid on the steaming pot and pushed the pot and the serving board to the center of the table. She chuckled at Silver's suggestion. "We have a whole room full of rock candy, Steven," she said. "Would you and Stearns care to see it?"

"I know I would," I blurted out. "Ginger —"

"Oh, I see," Ethel interrupted. "You two *have* been talking to your sister. She must've told you the most fantastic things. She and her friend Betsy are regular visitors, our only ones. A six-year-old has a wonderful imagination, you know. So impressionistic. Such a lovely age — six. Did she mention —"

"Soda pop coming out of the faucets!" Now it was my turn to interrupt.

"Goodness me!" Ethel exclaimed. At the opposite end of the table, Mad Maddie took time out from eating, which she did ravenously, one spoonful after another, to giggle. It was the first sound I'd heard her make, and I could feel the hairs on the back of my neck stand on end.

"Not faucets," Ethel exclaimed. "Casks. Small barrels, two in fact, with little spouts that pour out root beer. It's the first thing your sister and Betsy do when they come visiting — go right into the kitchen and pour themselves a drink. It's great fun. Like the spaghetti-eating plant."

"Then you do have one," I said.

"Oh, my, yes," said Ethel. "Why, just a moment ago, you were sitting next to it on the divan, Stearns."

Embarrassed, Silver and I stared at our bowls of soup.

Ethel looked from one to the other of us and said with a smile, "I think you young men already found it out."

"We did," admitted Silver. "Did you notice?"

"Notice what?"

"The blob of spaghetti," said Silver. "We ... I dropped it in, but it wouldn't eat it."

"Was it just plain spaghetti?"

"Yes."

"Then naturally it wouldn't eat it. It's a very particular plant. Comes from the other side of the world. Japan, I believe. Plain truth is it's spoiled. It only likes spaghetti with meat sauce on it. That's why we keep roundsteak handy."

"No wonder it went for my fingers," I said, but Silver was off in another direction, the one in which he wanted to be going all along — spiders. Spinning around in his seat, he said, "Miss Madeline, why did you leave a dead spider on my doorknob?"

Almost at once, Mad Maddie's face turned five shades of red. She trembled so that her hat fell backward off her head and her soup spoon flew out of her hand and clattered across the tabletop, banging into the pot in the center. At the other end of the table, Ethel had a coughing fit that ended in a wheezing gasp.

"Naughty girl," said Ethel, in a tone of voice that sounded like my father's when he was about to lose his temper. "You've been through the moving wall again, when I specifically told you not to. It's too dangerous. You may go to your room!"

Silver and I sat in embarrassed silence. Imagine talking to someone over seventy as if she were a child!

Without a sound, Mad Maddie rose from her seat at the table. I'd never seen a sadder face in my life. But wait! What was happening now?

For some reason (we were about to find out), a clod of dirt fell off a beam high above our heads, dropped like a stone, and, giving us all a start — "Goodness me!" said Ethel — landed with a loud "THUNK!" on the lid of the pot in the center of the table. What followed was a nightmare. A spider, like some prehistoric monster, came crashing down upon us; it, too, landed on the lid of the pot from where it had fallen — leaped! — from the ceiling.

"Lycosa!" Mad Maddie screamed, scaring me down to my socks. "Lycosa!"

However scared I was by the sound of her voice, I was a hundred times more scared by the creature at eye level before me. Hugely thick, black, and hairy as a clogged drain, it stood upright, waved a couple of its long legs in the air, and, as if sizing up the situation, took a leisurely walk once around the outside rim of the pot. It had a head as large and as round as a fist, reddish black and oozing wet, with a bright yellow stripe above three rows of dark eyes, one row on top of the other, and a ferocious mouth — the picture on the cover of Silver's book. Legs, mouth, head, eyes that were looking mesmerizingly at me.

"Lycosa!" Mad Maddie screamed again, only louder.

Maybe it was the sound or the vibrations of her voice that startled the spider into action. Whatever the reason, it sprang upward from the lid of the pot, stretched its legs in midair, and came down with a splash right in the middle of my half-eaten bowl of soup. There it stood, menacingly, long enough to catch its breath, knee-deep in the orange liquid.

"Someone do something!" said Ethel with alarm, but Silver was already on his feet. "Get up, Tramp!" he shouted at me. "Before it bites you." Too late. Closer and closer the spider came, high-stepping out of the soup, across the place mat, to the edge of the table, where it stood, poised, ready to spring at my face.

But Silver was too quick for it. For the second time that winter (remember the snowball on my bleeding tongue?) you could say that he saved my life. With a catlike lunge across the table, he swatted the ferocious beast with his weatherbeaten knapsack, knocking it and my bowl of soup across the room, where they crashed together in an orange and black heap in the corner.

Now it was Mad Maddie's turn to move. Sidestepping around the table, she hurried over to the spider, reached down, and, unbelievably, took hold of it with her bare hand. I was on my feet and out the door — "Forget the coats!" — in an instant, taking one last look behind me. There was Mad Maddie, thereafter known to me as "The Spider Lady," holding the wolf spider close to her face, cooing and patting it gently, as its eight legs squirmed frantically among her fingers, in an effort to free itself. Ethel was nowhere to be seen.

Job or no job, I knew I'd never set foot inside the crazy ladies' house again. Not for anything. Turned out I was wrong.

17
An Explanation—Sort of

WELL, OF COURSE, IT HAD ALL BEEN A HORRIBLE MIS-take. My mom and dad, upon hearing the ghastly details (blurted out in a whoosh of words by Silver and myself), dropped what they were doing and ran across the street to see for themselves, to make sure that the two old crows were really all right. They returned about half an hour later, laughing and poking and teasing each other like a couple of kids, carrying our winter coats.

So what was what? It seemed that the explanation was simpler than one would expect. Both Ethel and Mad Maddie were plant lovers — quite an understatement! To protect the plants from insects that would destroy them by eating their leaves, the two sisters, being old-fashioned, had decided to solve the problem in two decidedly old-fashioned ways. Outside, in the trees surrounding their house, they put up all different types of birdhouses and feeders. And every so often they purchased a new birdbath, which they had delivered and placed strategically on the grounds. Together the bird-houses, feeders, and baths were enough to attract almost every bird in the neighborhood to help protect their vegetable and flower garden. Some birds, it was true, tried to and did eat some of the planted seeds —

crows and the like. But, as my father said, "The benefits brought about by the insect eaters far outweighed the liabilities of the seed eaters."

Inside the house the two sisters used quite another method — spiders! Specifically the wolf spider ("Lycosa"), which was a feared enemy of all plant-killing insects. Normally, as you might imagine, they didn't let the wolf spiders wander freely about the house, but kept them securely in place inside the hot room, the greenhouse, for their most delicate plants. Besides being a healthy environment for plants, the greenhouse was also a perfect place to raise spiders. It was hot and damp, excellent wolf spider climate, and there was an abundance of rich soil in which to dig their nests and lay their eggs.

This arrangement — birds outside, spiders inside — had apparently been working just fine for many years. There were a few problems, mostly caused by the tremendous number of birds, which seemed to double in population every few years or so. In the summertime, so Ethel told my parents, the chirping, screeching, cawing, fussing, and flying about of all the birds made an enormous racket (the depth of the gully muted the noise you heard on the street), kept them awake at night, and generally made life quite uncomfortable. Still, Ethel didn't have the heart (or the strength?) to take down even a single one of the birdhouses or feeders, or dismantle the baths. For where would the birds go then? And who would protect their gardens?

On the other hand, inside the house, the spider population tended to regulate itself. Each year hundreds of tiny spider eggs were laid, hundreds of baby spiders hatched, hundreds died. Inside the greenhouse there just wasn't enough spider food — insects — to go around. Only the hardiest survived. Not only that, but wolf spiders, for want of food, ate each other as well. As a result, dead spiders of all sizes kept turning up among the plants in the greenhouse on a regular basis. It was Mad Maddie's job to take care of them, which she did enthusiastically. Spiders, after all, was her favorite hobby. (I noticed, as my mom and dad were recounting this tale, that Ethel failed to mention just what Mad Maddie was apt to do with some of the dead spiders she found.) So even though the spider collection had survived, even flourished, for years and years, it never got out of hand the way the birds did. There were never any more than two dozen wolfies living inside the greenhouse at any one time. And because of the fierce competition for survival, they tended to be the huge, hairy, hungry variety, like the ferocious one Silver and I had just seen.

Then one day, about two months ago, Mad Maddie had captured a live, female — pregnant — wolfie, and for some unexplainable reason (probably to play with on her bed, Ethel suspected) had taken it out of the hot room and into her own. Once there, she'd turned away for a second when — zip! — the spider was gone, off somewhere in the house to lay her eggs.

Mad Maddie looked everywhere, afraid to tell Ethel what she'd done. It was about six weeks later that the first young wolf spider turned up, crawling across

Ethel's lap as she sat reading the newspaper. Ethel herself refuses to touch the creatures. She shooed it away and called for her sister's help.

"Now how do you suppose he got in here?" she'd asked, but Mad Maddie said nothing.

The very next day it happened again — only twice. Two spiders turned up, one grubbing for bugs in the terrarium floor planter, the other galloping upside down across the ceiling, no doubt also in search of food. The truth was out, Mad Maddie confessed, and together the two sisters went in search of other newborn wolfies. All told, more than sixty spiders or their remains had been found, some by Ginger and Betsy, who were exceptionally fond of what they called "The Spider Hunt."

One spider they'd all searched very hard for, the mother spider, had never been found — that is until it burst upon the scene by falling into our lunch and scaring us all, except for Mad Maddie, half to death.

So there it was. In just a few minutes of Silver's and my time inside the crazy ladies' house and a short talk with my mom and dad, all the mysteries we'd been puzzling over had been cleared up, except two: the moving wall ("You've been through the moving wall again," Ethel had said.) and the reason for Mad Maddie's leaving dead spiders, some inside bottles of formaldehyde, all over the place. Silver dismissed the second mystery with a wave of his hand. "She's just nuts," he said. "It probably doesn't mean anything at all."

One final thing. Later, when my mom and I were by ourselves, I asked her if she wouldn't mind not serving me hot soup for a while. The mere thought of the mother wolf spider standing in my bowl of soup was enough to make me puke.

"I understand," she said. "But don't make too big a thing of it. It's awful, of course, and I'm sure it was frightening when it happened, but wolf spiders don't bite, no matter how fierce they look."

"According to Silver, they bite, and more."

"No doubt. Silver has a vivid imagination, which sometimes carries him away."

I changed the subject. "What's wrong with them, Mom?"

"Wrong? With whom?"

"The MacElvies. One of them — Maddie — seems crazy half the time, she wouldn't stop staring at Silver, and the other half like . . . like a little kid. That's it! About as old as Ginger. And Ethel, she's real friendly, smart too, but I don't know. She seems a bit crazy herself. All those plants and the rings and earring and the grandfather clock she talks about as if it were a person."

My mom smiled. "They're just getting old, Tramp. It's as simple as that. There's an old saying that if you live long enough you'll eventually return to your childhood ways. I think you see a touch of that with Madeline. Not Ethel though. From what I can tell, she's as sharp as can be. Eccentric but harmless, both of them, I assure you. They — Ethel — asked me to apologize for them. She hopes you and Silver will take on the gardening job, but she'll understand if you don't. I hope you take it."

"I can't speak for Silver," I said. "But as for me, I doubt it."

The image of Mad Maddie picking up the spider in her bare hands was still too clear in my mind. Vividly clear! And another thing. If there'd been sixty spiders roaming around, who says there wouldn't be sixty — or a thousand and sixty — more? Gardening? Not for me. No sir.

18
The Strangest Disease in the World

THE SILVER BULLET AND I DIDN'T SEE EACH OTHER for a long time after the fateful Saturday afternoon we'd spent at the crazy ladies' house. A day or two later his father loaded his suitcase in the family car and drove him back to Courtland, three hours away, where he'd spend two whole months, until his next school vacation in April.

As for myself, once I'd stopped dreaming about hairy spiders crawling under my sheets at night, my life became pretty normal, downright boring in fact. Basketball season ended and there was nothing more for me to look forward to. I guess it was mostly boredom that made me decide to try out for a spot in the school play.

The play was called "The Three Pink Leprechauns." And, no, it wasn't for little kids, even though it was a fairy tale, complete with witches, warlocks, a king and queen, a prince and princess, talking toadstools, leprechauns, and a lot of other supposedly magical creatures. It was really a musical, although the part I tried out for — and got! — was for one of the nonsinging leprechauns. (The play should've been called "The Six Pink Leprechauns," three singing and three nonsinging.) Why not a singing part for me? Simple. My singing voice sounded something like a dentist's drill under water.

Once I'd gotten the part, I found that I really liked it. Rehearsals were fun, especially when everyone's lines were memorized, and we could practice the play, act by act, without a lot of starting and stopping, or yelling and screaming by Mr. Allenweigle, the music teacher in charge of directing the play. I found that I enjoyed hamming it up on stage, knowing that when it was my turn to speak or laugh or dance about that other kids would be watching me, including a wicked witch named Sally West.

One day in late March, the first day of dress rehearsal, the strangest disease in the world took hold of me. Dress rehearsal meant, of course, practicing the play wearing costumes and make-up, using props and all the rest. Mr. Allenweigle instructed everyone to "Get the lead out!" and report, fully costumed, half an hour earlier than usual. That's probably why I forgot my gloves and hat inside my locker at school, which accounted for my second attack of the strangest disease in the world later on — but not the first.

Getting ready to be a pink leprechaun was no easy

matter. I found my costume (so did the five other leprechauns) stuffed inside a dirty box that Mr. Allenweigle had dragged out into the center of the boys' bathroom. It seemed that the costumes had been used in the same play some years before and stored down in the school basement, where they'd become moldy and rotten. After a mad scramble — during which Mr. Allenweigle kept shouting at the top of his lungs "Only two shoes to a customer!" — I managed to snatch an entire outfit for myself. Pink knickers, knee socks, jacket, rose-colored shirt, three-sided hat, and pointy pink slippers, each of which happened to fit snugly on my left foot.

A bit of trading followed: this jacket for that hat, this sock for that shoe, this pint-sized shirt for that jumbo one, this belt buckle for that whatchamacallit, and pretty soon nearly everyone was satisfied. As for my own damp and smelly costume, it was slightly on the small size, due to my elongated shape (I was, after all, just about the tallest kid in the seventh grade, easily the tallest leprechaun). Oh, well, nobody's perfect.

After we were dressed in our costumes, it was make-up time. Mr. Allenweigle demonstrated how to apply the make-up, using the littlest kid he could find as a guinea pig. Actually, there was nothing to it. You just opened a jar of greasy pink paste, gouged out a globful with your hand, and smeared it all over your face — everywhere skin showed. When it was my turn, I sucked in my breath, shut my eyes, and — splat! — slapped it all over my face. Between the foul odor of my long-dead costume and the sticky odor of the make-up, I must've smelled like one of the grossest human beings in the world. Still, I loved it, in part because there were five other leprechauns looking and smelling exactly as I did.

The rehearsal, it turned out, ran as smoothly as could be, much more so than we'd ever done it before. I guess that was only natural, seeing how everyone was dressed up, excited, and determined not to mess up. Also, probably in the back of everybody's mind (as it was in mine) was the thought that our first performance in front of an audience was less than a week away.

The play was divided into five acts. All my lines were delivered in the first act and the last. After the first act, I'd gotten into the habit of leaving the stage, walking to the rear of the auditorium, and standing in the dark where I could watch the second, third, and fourth acts undisturbed. Mostly, however, I just watched Sally. Her part, that of a wicked old witch, took place in the second and fourth acts, so I had a good chance to watch her as she stalked around the stage, grumbling and snapping and taking out her evil ways on the helpless toadstools, the kind-hearted princess, and any other character who had the misfortune to cross her path.

It was strange to see Sally in that role, exciting, too, because it was so different from how she really was — gentle, quiet (except when she was blowing her nose), and considerate. Her traditional witch's costume consisted of a pitch-black dress, cone-shaped hat, thick-soled shoes, three-inch-long purple fingernails, crooked nose, and for special effect, a handful of ugly brown warts spread all over her face. I noticed that whenever her part was over and she was no longer on stage, she was quick to remove the warts and the wrinkly beak of a nose. But if she did that because she was worried about how she looked, she needn't have. Anyone with half a brain could tell that beneath those ugly props and all that make-up was one pretty girl.

Standing by myself in the back of the darkened auditorium, watching Sally and the rest of the kids practicing act two, I had a sudden, and I guess you'd call it romantic, idea. What if, by some miracle, Sally should do exactly as I had — leave the stage (she wasn't in act three), wander through the dark, and end up standing right next to me? What would I do? Why, the only thing I could do under the circumstances: put my arm around her, turn her in my direction, bend down, and — warts or no warts, beak nose or no beak nose — kiss her ever so gently on the lips. It's what she'd want me to do, I was sure of it. After all, hadn't we danced together? And talked? Didn't I still have her phone number and address in my wallet? It wasn't as if we were strangers, was it? No, it wasn't.

While I'd been off in my dream world, act two had come to a close, props and scenery rearranged, and act three begun. Before I knew what was happening, a soft, swishing noise sounded a little way off to one side of me. Someone was coming! And I didn't have to look twice to know who it was. Silhouetted by the lights from the brightened stage, gliding along beneath a cone-shaped witch's hat, her long dress swaying to and fro up the aisle, came Sally.

Was it a dream? A mirage? Uh-uh. It was Sally, no doubt about it, moving as gracefully as she always moved — and straight in my direction.

When she reached the last row of seats, she stopped. Taking her time, she removed the awkward witch's hat, pulled off the ridiculous nose, and plucked the warts from her face. She put all three — hat, nose, warts — on the aisle seat, smoothed back her long hair, and came closer, right next to where I was standing. Our two arms touched.

Again a wave of panic swept over me, exactly as it had four months ago, the moment before I'd first asked Sally to dance. My adam's apple, large as a coconut, lodged in my throat. My entire body stiffened, rigid as a totem pole. I stared straight ahead, not daring to move. Had she seen me? Did she know that I was there? Had she deliberately come back to be near me? Or was it just by chance that she'd come to the rear of the auditorium and happened to find me?

Neither of us moved, neither of us spoke. Then just as suddenly as my body'd become rigid, it began to relax. My racing heart slowed to its normal beat, my muscles loosened, my adam's apple reverted to its usual size. I could turn my head from side to side. I could breathe. I, Tramp Steamer, was not about to repeat my past mistakes. "Of course she knows you're here, idiot!" I said to myself. "That's why she's here. Now put your arm around her and do what you have to do, what she wants you to do. Kiss her."

It was all so simple. Only it wasn't. The strangest disease in the world had taken hold of my arm, the one touching Sally's. As relaxed and confident as I was feeling, nothing I could do would make my arm budge an inch, never mind rise high enough to put around Sally. A terrible paralysis had taken hold of it. Try as I might, it stayed fastened to my side, in the same rigid position it'd been in all along. "Come on!" I said to myself. "Before it's too late."

But it already was. With a barely audible sigh and a swish of her skirt, Sally moved off, collected her belongings, and was on her way back to the stage and act four. The strange paralysis had caused me to miss another opportunity with the girl I spent practically all my time daydreaming about.

Using my healthy arm, I reached across my body and gave my paralyzed wrist a sharp tug. To my surprise, the wrist and arm moved easily and without resistance. I gave it a shake to make sure. It was perfectly capable of moving fine on its own. Just as quickly as it had come, the strangest disease in the world had gone without a trace.

19
An Unexpected Turn of Events

"WANT TO WALK ME HOME, OBE?"

For a second I couldn't believe my ears. Was this really Sally West, practically the most popular girl in the seventh grade, the same girl before whom I'd made a miserable fool of myself just moments ago, standing outside the auditorium door in the cold and dark, waiting for me? It was.

What a stroke of luck!

"Sh-sure," I stammered, buttoning my coat and fumbling inside my pockets for the pair of gloves and hat that weren't there.

"Forget something?" Sally asked.

"No," I said and kept my hands inside my pockets. "It's nothing."

Together we began to walk away from the school, along a well-lighted road that ran straight through the center of town, directly past Sally's house. For late March, the weather was downright annoying — bitter cold, well below freezing. About every five seconds the wind would rise up and blast us in our faces. Sally tugged her woolen ski hat down over her ears. If I'd been by myself, with the guys, or anyone else but Sally, I'd have gone back to the school before the custodians locked it up, and gotten my gloves and hat from where I'd left them inside my locker. But with Sally that was out of the question. What if I asked her to head back to school and she said no? Then where would I be? As it was, I didn't even have the nerve to slow down for a moment and pull up the collar on my coat.

It was lucky for me that Sally was such a good talker, because if the talking had been left up to me, I knew I'd have been a flop. Our walk home would've been long and embarrassingly silent. But Sally talked, on and on in fact, about dress rehearsal, her trouble memorizing her lines, school the next day, homework, teachers, what it was like moving to a new town, never once letting me get a word in edgewise. Not that I wanted to! Even now I was on guard, not wanting to make a fool of myself. The less I said the better.

For some reason, her calling me Obe made me feel older, more grown up. I wanted to ask her how she came to know my middle name and why she chose to call me by a former nickname instead of my current one, but I knew that I lacked the courage. Funny, at first I thought her constant chatter was to make up for my almost total silence (I managed to grunt now and then) or that she was freezing cold and talking to stay warm. But then I had another thought, altogether different. Maybe she was the one who was scared — well, not scared as much as nervous — with her jittery talk, speeding from one topic to the next, stumbling over her words, with barely a breath in between. Sure, she still spoke with the same soft, flute-sounding voice, but she was talking in such a strange way for Sally West. And she wasn't asking me any questions. That was strange, too. Then all at once she startled me by saying, "You're lucky to have so many friends, Obe."

"Me!" I said, practically shouting. "You're the one with all the friends."

She started to say something, but stopped short. Our walking slowed down a bit. For the first time since we'd left the auditorium she became silent, thoughtful. "Oh, no!" I said to myself, beginning to wish that I were somewhere else. "You've said something wrong. Nice going, idiot!"

"I hang around a lot of kids," I mumbled, trying to

make up for lost ground. "But I really don't have many friends. Only one. And you don't even know him."

"What's his name?" Sally asked, surprised.

"Sil — Steven Branch," I said. "He goes to boarding school."

"I've heard of him," she said. "Wasn't he at the Thanksgiving dance?"

"Uh-huh."

"Why do you like him?"

"Why?" It was an unusual question. She was back to being the Sally I knew.

"Yes, why?" she asked again.

"I don't know," I said. "He's different . . . we've done a lot of things together . . . we live on the same street."

"But you must like him for reasons other than those."

I shrugged. "I'm his best friend."

Sally laughed. Not a mean laugh, a friendly one. It almost made me forget the winter cold.

"I'm sorry," she said. "When you get to know me, you'll see how annoying I can be."

"You're not annoying," I said.

"Yes," she said, "I am."

"Why do you call me Obe?" I asked.

"It's a nice name. I learned about it from some of the kids at school. They all know you."

"They should," I said. "I've lived here all my life."

After that, we walked along in silence. Only it was a different kind of silence this time, because neither of us was so caught up in trying to think of what to say. I know that I wasn't. I pulled my collar up until it half-covered my ears. Every so often a car would go by on the street, honk its horn, and once some older kids yelled something that sounded like "lovers!" out the car window. That embarrassed me some, but mostly I liked it.

The rest of the way to Sally's house I concentrated on what I was going to do once we got there. Was I going to kiss her, shake her hand, say goodnight, or what? She began to hum some of the songs from the musical we'd just finished practicing, and I was quick to notice that when she sang she had an even more beautiful voice than when she simply spoke. I wondered why Mr. Allenweigle, the jerk, hadn't given her a singing part in the play.

Stealthily, I took my hand from my pocket, the one next to Sally. Exposed to the bitter night air, it took no time for it to freeze up and begin to ache, along with my nose and partially protected ears. I had a vague notion to take hold of Sally's hand, but when I tried to stretch out my fingers and accidentally on purpose bump them into Sally's, as her gloved hand gently swung back and forth, I found that neither my fingers nor my hand would budge an inch. For the second time that day the strangest disease in the world had struck, only this time in my opposite hand. What was I to do? I waited until the attack passed and I was able to slip my hand back inside my pocket.

About five minutes later we passed the fire station and arrived at Sally's house. It felt funny — in a good way! — walking up her front steps, something I'd thought of doing about a million times, but never dreamed that I would, and after walking Sally home from school, no less. She had a nice front porch, protected by tall evergreens, complete with rocking chairs and a hammock that was whipping frantically in the wind.

I'd put kissing her out of my mind. If I didn't have the courage to put my arm around her or hold her hand, I wasn't going to kid myself by thinking I'd have the courage to kiss her goodnight. A wave would do, for the time being, no sense pressing my luck. Besides, I was already floating several yards above the ground.

Sally opened her front door. A stream of bright light shot out and lit up our faces. The sound of friendly laughter, piano playing, and children whooping and squealing filtered out from inside the house. Suddenly, Sally turned to face me. "Well," she said, her face staring up into mine. "Are you gonna kiss me or not?"

"I . . . I . . . I . . ."

I couldn't move, but it didn't matter. *She* kissed *me.* Took my cheeks in both her gloved hands, pulled my face down, and kissed me, pushing her squishy lips into my own. It wasn't a long kiss, but it wasn't a short one either. It was a perfectly warm and wonderful kiss, a kiss that made my ears defrost, my skin itch, my heart leap and toss about like a rock band.

Then she was gone. But not before pulling off her woolen hat, stuffing it into my hand, and saying, "Stretch this over your head. You'll need it on the way home. Goodnight."

Like a hot-air balloon, I floated down the steps and about halfway to the sidewalk when Sally's front door opened again. "I *hang around* a lot of kids, too," she shouted. "Don't forget that, Obe. See ya!"

I didn't forget. I knew exactly what she meant.

20
Preparing for Tadpoles

EXCEPT FOR ONE PROBLEM, WHICH CAME UP LATER, the month of April was one of the best months of my entire life. Overnight the weather blossomed into spring. "The Three Pink Leprechauns" turned out to be a fun success, if you didn't count the stray dog that ran back and forth across the stage during act one, or the scenery that fell apart midway through the final act. Also, I turned thirteen and got a new AM-FM portable radio from my parents and a turtleneck sweater from Sally.

Speaking of Sally, I began to spend more and more time with her. We ate lunch in the cafeteria, walked home after school, did homework together. One weekend I took her to see a movie, science fiction. Inside the movie theater, when I tried to put my arm around her, I learned that I'd rid myself of the strangest disease in the world. I also learned that her porch was a wonderful place to sit together (when it was warm!) day or night, especially when her parents and her little brothers weren't around. We were getting to know each other well, and by the end of April, I was spending so much time at Sally's house that I didn't even notice the day The Silver Bullet came home to start his spring vacation.

But then there he was, pounding on my bedroom window early one Saturday morning, before I'd even had a chance to wake up.

"What've you been up to?" he asked, once I'd let him in the back door.

"Oh, nothing," I said, yawning and flopping back down on my bed. "How've you been?"

"Terrific," he said with more than a usual note of sarcasm. He looked pale and hollow-eyed, as if he'd spent the last few months in a basement and without much sleep. "Exams are all over this term. I thought you'd come by last night, like you always do the nights I get home. What'd you do, forget?"

"No." I lied. "I was . . . busy, that's all."

Silver looked at me hard, then shrugged. "No matter. I was too tired to do anything anyway — exams and all. What's going on today?"

"Today!" I shouted, jumping up. "I almost forgot. I've got to help Ginger and her friend . . ."

"Betsy?"

"Yeah, Betsy. They've got to catch some tadpoles for a school science project. My mom asked me to go along with them to the frog pond. She thinks it's too dangerous for them to go alone. Besides, by themselves they probably wouldn't catch anything."

"Don't be too sure," said Silver. "What frog pond?

The one inside the forest preserve, near the old car . . ."

The mere mention of the dreaded place near Dead Man's Shoot caused the inside of my mouth to begin hurting all over again. Silver knew exactly what I was thinking.

"Tongue still hurt?" he said, grinning. But it wasn't the old grin, the one I was used to seeing flash across his face. Half that, no more.

"Very funny," I said. "No, not that place. Noddle's Pond. The one behind the auto body shop."

"It's polluted," said Silver. "You sure there're frogs there?"

"Used to be."

"Yeah, before they built the highway and the shopping center."

"You don't have to come," I said, though I very much wanted him to. I'd be less embarrassed catching tadpoles with two six-year-olds if Silver came along. "I'm just telling you what *I* have to do today."

"Touchy, very touchy," said Silver. "Just give me a moment to go home and get my knapsack and I'll be back and have some breakfast with you. Tell your mom I haven't had pancakes in a long while, will you?" And with that he was gone.

Ginger and Betsy came prepared. Starting out, I was astonished to see the two of them struggling down the driveway on either side of an enormous box. Apparently the box was so heavy that to carry it each of them had to stoop over and hold on to the handles with both hands.

Silver and I nearly fell down laughing. They looked like two crabs dragging a huge chunk of food along the beach. Two or three times they had to put the box down and rest a minute — all before reaching the end of the driveway.

"At this rate, we'll get to Noddle's Pond by next Christmas," said Silver. "When all the frogs'll be frozen to death."

"What's in the box, girls?" I asked.

"Something," said Ginger.

Betsy giggled. A little bead of sweat dripped off her nose.

"Oh, come on, Ginger," I said. "We'll find out anyway once we get to the pond."

The two girls looked at each other. Neither of them spoke.

Silver stepped in. "Tramp and I'll carry it for you," he said. "Otherwise, once we got there, you two'd be too tired to do anything, forget catching tadpoles."

Ginger was stubborn, but she was no dope.

"Okay," she said reluctantly. "Only no peeking inside."

"We won't have to peek inside," said Silver. "Before we pick this thing up and carry it a step, you're going to tell us what we're carrying. Isn't that right, Tramp?"

"Fair's fair," I said. "Is it a deal?"

Ginger and Betsy looked at each other.

"It's a deal," said Ginger. "But you got to promise not to tell Mom. I borrowed some of her jars."

"Jars?" I said. "You mean preserving jars?"

Ginger nodded.

"How many?" I said.

"Cross your heart and never fear, stick your finger in your ear."

"Gingcr!"

"Go on," she said. "Do it and promise."

Like a fool, I did it, to get going more than anything else. "Promise," I said. "But Ginger, Mom probably wouldn't mind you taking a few."

"You too," she said, turning to Silver.

He crossed his heart, stuck his finger in his ear, and said with feigned seriousness, "I promise." I could tell that he was feeling better.

"Twenty-one," said Ginger.

"Twenty-one!" I shouted. "You took twenty-one of Mom's best preserving jars?"

"Yep," said Ginger.

"Why so many?"

"One for everyone in the class, including Miss Davenport, my teacher, and me and Betsy."

"Your sister takes after me," said Silver, much amused. "Only, I'd have let old Miss Davenport get her own tadpoles."

"I don't get it, Ginger," I said. "You can catch all the tadpoles you want and put them *all* in one jar. You don't need a jar for every tadpole."

"I know that," said Ginger. "We need the jars for the pond water."

"Makes sense," said Silver, chuckling under his breath.

"Well, let's go," I said, grabbing onto one of the handles. "No sense wasting an entire morning arguing."

21
A Tale of Two Ponds

NODDLE'S POND (WHO MR. OR MRS. NODDLE WAS was anybody's guess), like many other places in town, had done a lot of changing. Before the highway and shopping center had been built, the pond was a cool, friendly spot, part of a park, set off by clumps of shady trees, including an old willow that dipped its stately branches into the water. Springtime found the water clear and cold (not good for swimming, though — too many snakes!) and the pond almost always full because of the tremendous thaw. By midsummer the water had become warm and murky with unsettled mud and floating algae, and alive with birds, frogs, toads, salamanders, turtles, crayfish, bees and beetles, snakes, catfish, dragonflies, ducks, an occasional rat or two, even, on one occasion, a family of opossum. It was the greatest place in the world for catching things, including poison ivy.

Then the highway was built, an interstate, and after that a shopping center. What a difference! Practically overnight, the trees were cut down (all but the old willow — Silver used to claim that it was invisible to anyone who'd even think of cutting it down), stumps pulled up and hauled away, gravel and sand dumped, tar poured and smoothed and left to harden. What great fun it'd been to get up early, hurry down to Noddle's before school, sit on top of the huge sand banks, and watch the men and their machinery making a terrific racket, an avalanche of noise. What fun, except for one thing: when it was all over and the men and their machines had left, the pond was gone, or most of it anyway. So was the park, its animal life, plants, insects, fish, and birds. A thousand sounds — chirps, snorts, hoots, howls, splashes, peeps, croaks, grunts, snarls, screeches, caws, quacks — had been replced by the continuous noise of the highway traffic and the cars pulling in and out of the nearby auto body shop's parking lot.

Good thing we still had the forest preserve!

Carrying the box between us, it took Silver and me and the girls (who hurried on a block ahead) about ten minutes to reach what was left of Noddle's Pond. It was worse than I remembered, littered with broken glass, aluminum cans, rubbish, gravel, the usual filth. An ugly layer of yellow foam floated on the surface of the shallow water. A rubber tire stuck up out of the water beneath the overhanging willow tree, which had taken on a sickly, withered look, its branches no longer touching the water.

"Disgusting," said Silver, surveying the scene.

But no matter what Silver and my feelings were about the place, Ginger and Betsy seemed unperturbed. No sooner had we dropped the box at our feet than they came scurrying around from the opposite side of the pond, tore open the lid of the box, and began removing the jars, one by one, as well as two miniature fishnets.

"Bet you don't find any tadpoles," I said.

"Yeah," Silver agreed. "Besides us, the only thing living around here is the garbage." He swung his knapsack off his shoulders and put it on the ground. "But I brought along my own equipment just in case."

Ginger barely gave either of us a look. She and Betsy were too busy getting ready. As for Silver, he opened his knapsack, pulled out a net identical to the others, only bigger, and his own jar, complete with air holes punched into the lid. "Thought I'd help out," he said, giving me a wink.

"We don't need any help," said Ginger. "We've already found more tadpoles than we need."

"What!"

I was incredulous. Silver looked at my face and gave a big laugh. "Show me, Gin," he said.

The two little girls led us to the other side of the pond, near the shoulder of the highway. There, in between a few sparse yellow reeds, were at least fifty healthy-looking tadpoles, each an inch long, swimming about in water no deeper than a bathtub.

"How'd you know where to look?" I asked.

"Me and Betsy have been here before . . ." Ginger said. She stopped abruptly, realizing her mistake. "Don't tell Mommy, Tramp. Please. Promise you won't tell? Please."

"I've sure done a lot of promising today," I said, noticing that she'd called me Tramp, not Pole. "But don't worry, I won't tell. Just don't come back by yourself again. It's not all that safe. Okay?"

"Okay," said Ginger, but I could tell by her voice that she didn't entirely mean it. Who was I to be bossing her around?

It took the two girls about half an hour to catch the tadpoles, put one or two inside each jar, and fill the jars with pond water. Silver, meanwhile, was up to his old tricks, stalking around the edge of the pond, then checking on something he'd spotted near the back of the auto body shop, a bare brick wall. While the three of them went about their business, I sat under the willow tree, out of the hot sun, and watched the trucks on the highway gearing up for their run up the steep incline. I was thinking about the great time I was going to have with Sally and her family. They'd invited me to go with them to their cabin in the mountains. Five whole days, almost the entire spring vacation, with Sally, swimming in a lake, fishing, boating, hiking — we were to leave first thing in the morning.

"Hey-o!" Silver shouted. "Look what I found."

"What is it?" I called out, too comfortable to move.

"Never seen one," he answered. "Some kind of nest or something. It looks like a couple of mud baseball bats."

Mud baseball bats? Whatever it was, it rated a look.

"Mud daubers," Ginger announced when we were all standing before it. Silver was right. It did look like a couple of mud baseball bats, two long crusty-brown tubes baking in the sun, partially hidden by a rotten log. I wondered if the tubes were hollow.

"What're mud daubers?" Silver asked.

"Wasps," said Ginger. "It's a wasp nest."

"Good thing it's all dried up," I said.

"It only looks that way," said Ginger. "Because it's a year old. The wasp eggs take a year to hatch. When they're ready they'll make a door and come flying out."

"How do you know?" I asked, amazed at my little sister's knowledge.

"Miss Davenport read us about it in a book."

"Let's poke a hole in it," said Silver, "to help the wasps get started."

"No!" the two little girls shouted at the same time. "No," said Ginger. "Leave nature's work to itself. Miss Davenport says so."

Again, I was amazed.

"But you're disturbing tadpoles," said Silver.

"But that's . . . that's . . . only for a few weeks," said Ginger.

Silver was about to argue, but I cut him off.

"Look," I said. "We got what we came for. It's too hot to stay here any longer than we have to. Let's get going."

Silver shrugged. "Sure thing," he said. "Besides, I wasn't going to hurt them, Gin. Just experiment a little."

Getting going, it turned out, was easier said than done. With all twenty-one jars filled with pond water, the box had become impossibly heavy to carry, even for the two of us. To make matters worse, in trying to pick it up, one of the handles broke. We ended up calling my dad for a ride.

While we waited for him, an unusual-looking car pulled into the nearby parking lot, sped in was more like it, making a lot of noise. The outside of the car looked like one of those New York City subways, spray-painted a hundred different colors — even the hubcaps were green. One whole side was smashed in, the windshield was cracked. A raccoon's head was mounted on the dashboard.

When the car had stopped, both doors opened at once and four boys, high school kids, piled out. One of them, the driver, was a big, muscular kid, wearing a white T-shirt and jeans. A leather cowboy hat was cocked on the back of his head. He was holding on to a jittery looking Doberman pinscher on a chain leash.

My heart stopped beating. I took a look at Silver. "Looks different without his ski mask," he said.

22
A Waspy Revenge

SKI MASK ATTACHED THE LEASH TO THE DOOR HANdle on the driver's side of the car. Then he and his friends elbowed and shoved their way across the lot, toward the auto body shop, laughing and punching one another in the arms, while behind them the dog barked wildly and strained to break its leash.

"Hey!" my dad shouted, pulling up to the curb behind us and giving us all a start. "Anybody want a ride?"

It took a moment, but with my dad's help, we loaded the box full of tadpoles and pond water onto the back seat. Ginger and Betsy sat guarding it on either side. I slammed the car door after them.

"Climb in front, fellas," said my dad. "I'm in a bit of a hurry."

"Go on without us, Dad," I said. "Silver and I have some business to finish up here."

My dad gave us a quizzical smile. "See you later," he said and drove off.

I turned to look at Silver, who greeted me with a satisfied grin from ear to ear. His dazzling smile was back.

"What're you grinning at?" I said irritably.

"Nothing," he said. "I was hoping you'd send them on their way without my suggesting it, that's all."

"Got a plan?" I said, motioning toward the psychedelic car and the barking Doberman.

"Of course," said Silver. "Come on. There's no time to lose."

He was headed around back of the building.

"Mud daubers!" I exclaimed.

"Right you are," he said, picking up a stick and breaking it in two. He knelt down before the crusty-brown nest. "You start digging at that end, and be careful. We don't want this thing to come apart in our hands."

We set to work at once and managed, without too

much difficulty, to pry the nest loose from its dirt and log foundation, keeping it perfectly intact.

"Grab on to your end," Silver said. "I know you're not going to believe this, but we're going to hide this time bomb underneath the back seat of that overgrown musclehead's car."

He was right. I didn't believe it.

Carrying the cylindrical nest and the layer of dirt beneath it turned out to be easier than expected. True, the sun-dried nest was extremely fragile and bulky, but it was also light. Each of us taking up an end, we shuffled out from behind the building and across the parking lot toward Ski Mask's car. There was only one problem: the Doberman saw us coming. Straining at its leash, it began at once to growl and bark, loud enough to wake the dead.

Silver, startled by the noise, veered sharply away from the entrance to the auto body shop, causing me to stumble and let go of the nest. It crashed in a dusty heap on the pavement. "Pick it up, quick," said Silver. I did, and together we carried it over to one side of the parking lot and set it down between two parked cars, out of the Doberman's sight. Three or four customers came out of the shop, passed right by us, got in their cars and drove off. When they'd gone, we inspected the damage.

A tiny opening split the center of the nest. Already a medium-sized black-and-yellow wasp was poking its way out of the opening. Popping free, it crawled in a circle on the dry surface of the nest, spread its wings, and flew off over our heads in the breeze.

"At least we know they're alive," said Silver. We watched another wasp push its way out of the nest.

"What do we do now?" I said.

"Nothing," said Silver. "Even if we could get inside the car the Doberman would make so much noise that the jerks'd come running for sure."

But I wasn't about to give up, not for anything. The memory of Dead Man's Shoot and my bloody tongue was still too clear in my mind.

"Maybe . . ." I began. "I got it! You got any food?"

Of course he had.

"Only a tuna fish and salami sandwich," he said, his face brightening. "And a pickle."

"Feed it to the dog!" we both said at the same time. Amazing how two old friends could think along the same lines.

"Okay," said Silver. "You feed. I'll plant the nest under the back seat."

"You feed, I'll plant," I said.

Once again his face burst into a smile. He slapped my back. "Tramp," he said. "You sure have come a long way. Stick with me and there's no telling how far you'll go."

"Cut the crap," I said. "We've got to move fast. They'll be coming out soon. Whatever you do, don't run out of sandwich while I'm still inside the car."

"Whatever *you* do," he said, "don't let the wasps bite your head off."

"Very funny."

The only way for me to carry the wasps' nest by myself was to slide my hands and arms beneath the middle of it, palms upward, and hug it against my chest. Silver had put a glob of spit on top of the tiny opening to temporarily prevent any wasps from escaping. It worked, but not for long.

As soon as the Doberman spotted us sneaking up behind the car, it bared its teeth in a fierce growl. But the sight and smell of Silver's tuna fish and salami sandwich made it shut up in a hurry. Its growl became a whimper, it wagged its tail in short jerks and began drooling and pawing the hot pavement.

"Nice doggy," said Silver.

I made my move, skirting past Silver and on to the passenger side of the car. There I set the nest down, opened the door, pushed the front seat forward, and climbed inside. At once, I was struck by the smell of cigarette smoke, the sight of ashtrays stuffed with moldy cigarette butts, the raccoon's face staring at me from the dashboard, the piles of crushed beer cans littering the floor, front and back. Where was I? Inside the car of a group of guys, any one of whom was big and tough enough to beat my brains out and would, no problem, if he found me there.

The heat inside the car was terrific. Sweat poured out of every pore in my body, soaking me in an instant. Through the window, I could see Silver breaking off chunks of sandwich and tossing them at the Doberman, who was lapping them up, fast as could be. Then — horrors! — I saw something else: Ski Mask and his three friends coming out the door of the auto body shop.

Every one of my muscles was poised and ready to

run, but I was determined. These guys had caused me pain, bad pain. With all my might, I tugged the back seat and pulled it loose, sliding it forward onto the back floor. Reaching outside, I scooped up the wasp's nest and hugged it to my chest. But by this time Silver's spit had dried up. A king-sized wasp struggled through the opening, zeroed in on my nose, and zoomed forward. I closed my eyes and ducked. Zap! The wasp struck my forehead, bounced off, and flew into the air. There was no time to lose. Already another wasp was climbing through the hole, made larger by the fatty that had just pushed its way through.

I wheeled around. Ski Mask and his friends were now halfway across the lot, pushing and tugging at one another like a bunch of wrestlers and making a lot of noise. Silver saw them, too. He shot me a look through the window and gave me the scram sign with his thumb. No dice. Not until I was finished.

Quick as I could, I dumped the crumbly nest into the space beneath the back seat. Two wasps popped out, buzzed past my ear and out the door. There was only the back seat to put in place and I'd be gone. I gave it a yank. It didn't move. It had slid aside so easily. What was wrong? I pulled with all my strength, but it just wouldn't move. I could hear Ski Mask's voice clearly now. Silver gave me one last frantic warning — a horrified face at the window — before ducking down, out of sight. I was on my own. I gave a last frantic tug at the seat, looked up to see four shadows on the windshield. Too late. I was a goner.

No, I wasn't. Without warning, Ski Mask and his

friends came to an abrupt halt, did a complete about-face, and began to run in four different directions at the same time, whooping and shouting, all over the parking lot.

Whatever they were up to I didn't care. It was time to get going. I climbed out of the car and as an afterthought gave the back seat one more tug. As if by magic, it slid easily into place, concealing the wasp's nest beneath it. I pushed the front seat back and closed the door. The trap was set. I looked around for Silver, but both he and the Doberman were gone. What had happened?

"Psssst!" said a voice. It was Silver, on his stomach behind some nearby bushes. "Over here," he said. "Hurry!"

I did, and not a moment too soon. Ski Mask, his friends, and the Doberman on its chain leash emerged from behind the building and, once again, were heading for the car. I had just enough time to duck down next to Silver, out of sight.

We held our breath and listened. On the other side of the bushes there were voices, angry voices, car doors opening and slamming shut. From inside the car, a muffled voice growled, "Now how the hell did he get loose and not even bust his chain?" Then there was the roar of an engine, the screech of tires, and they were gone — sitting on a keg of waspy dynamite.

The two of us leaped to our feet and cheered. We grabbed on to each other's shoulders and jumped up and down in a circle, my knees wobbling with relief. We'd done it! And did it feel good!

"What kept you so long, Tramp? Were you taking a nap inside there?"

"Er . . . no. I couldn't get the stupid seat back in place. I was . . . er . . . kneeling on it."

Silver howled with laughter.

"After you untied the Doberman, how'd you get it to run all the way across the parking lot?" I asked.

"Guess."

"Come on," I implored.

"Simple," he said. "I threw the pickle."

Now it was my turn to howl. In fact, we both laughed long and hard all the way home. We decided it'd been worth the risk, every bit of it. The only bad part was that we wouldn't be there to see Ski Mask's face every time ten or twenty wasps flew out of nowhere and bit his behind off. But, nevertheless, it was still good — a good waspy revenge.

On our way home, Silver said, "What a great day for us, Tramp. A perfect way to begin spring vacation. I've made a lot of plans I want to tell you about, things that'd be good to do, now that I'm home. Come by tonight and I'll fill you in . . ."

"Hold on, Silver," I said. "I'm not going to be here."

"Tonight?"

"No, I'll be here tonight. It's the next five days I won't, until next Thursday. I met this girl, Sally, and her parents invited me up to their cabin in the mountains. Fishing, boating, hiking and all. It's going to be great!"

"Yeah, great," said Silver, a lot less excited than I

wanted him to be. "Sally, huh? Isn't she the girl you were dancing with at Thanksgiving?"

"Yeah, she's pretty and nice . . ."

"If you say so," said Silver. "I didn't get too good a look at her."

"You will," I said. "Anyway, I'll come by tonight. We can make plans for when I return."

"Oh, yeah," said Silver absently. "Tonight."

But I didn't see him that night. After dinner, when I went over to his house, he wasn't there. The lights in his room were on, but the door was locked — strange! — for the first time ever. And no one answered my knocks. He must've been out somewhere with his father. I didn't see him when I returned five days later from the trip with Sally and her parents either. My mom told me that she'd heard that Silver'd gone to spend some time in the city with his mother, but that was strange, too. He told me the day of the wasps that he'd seen his mother the weekend before, that she was moving out of state, and that from now on he wouldn't be seeing her as often. Oh, well. Plans do change.

23
Leave It to The Silver Bullet

THE NEXT TIME I SAW SILVER WAS IN EARLY JUNE, when his boarding school let out for the summer. (I, unfortunately, still had three weeks of school to go.) He found me one Saturday on my back porch, where I was eating a bowl of vanilla ice cream and watching my older brother, Tommy, at work on his car, a dark-blue, secondhand Volvo, boxy looking from the outside, but real roomy inside. It had red leather seats, a stick shift, and a new tape deck my brother'd installed himself under the dashboard. A few rust spots showed on the body and there was a three-foot-long scratch on the hood, but Tommy said that what counted most was the engine — a good one.

Silver looked terrible, even worse than the last time I'd seen him. For one thing, he was downright dirty, his hair and clothes a rumpled mess, as if he hadn't washed or changed in a couple of weeks. He'd lost some weight, his face was lean and pale — vanilla ice cream pale — which made his eyes seem large and black and tired-looking. Watching him come slowly up the driveway, I thought about the night his bedroom light was on with the door locked. It wasn't the time to find out why.

"Welcome to the summer," I said, feeling awkward. "Want some ice cream?"

He pulled up a chair and sat down. "No, thanks," he said. "New car?"

"My brother just bought it."

"Not bad," he said.

"How was school?" I said.

He gave me a hard look. "The usual bore," he said. "How's your girlfriend, whatshername?"

"Sally," I said. I began to tell him about my trip to her parents' cabin in the mountains, but I could tell that he wasn't interested.

A moment later my brother came up the porch steps, on his way into the house.

"How's the car?" I asked him.

"Good," he said, "except the trunk won't close all the way. Something's wrong with the lock. I had to use some rope to tie it down. Hi, Silver. What truck hit you?"

"Very funny," said Silver without changing his expression.

"Sorry," said Tommy, and he disappeared into the house.

"What's your brother doing tonight?" Silver said.

"Going out with Ellen, his girlfriend, I guess."

"Where do you think they'll go?"

"How should I know, Silver? Where would you go if you were seventeen and had a girl and a car?"

He didn't answer me. He was thinking hard about something. "Let's take a look at the trunk," he said.

I followed him down the porch steps and across the driveway, to where Tommy's car was parked in the shade. Silver knelt down and inspected the knot my brother had tied to keep the trunk down. One end of the rope was wound around the bumper, the other looped around the broken latch, inside the trunk. The knot was fastened securely, but not so that it couldn't be untied with a little effort.

"What's up, Silver?"

"Just this," he said. "Wherever your brother and his girlfriend go tonight, we're going to go, too. Unless, of course, you're busy."

"I'm not busy," I said, giving him a sarcastic look. "But what's Tommy going to do, invite us along? Or do we ride behind his car on our bicycles?"

Then it hit me. The trunk. Silver saw that I knew and smiled, the half-smile of a person who had a lot on his mind.

"It won't work," I said automatically.

"If I explain how, will you do it?" he said.

"Explain first. Then I'll tell you ten good reasons why we shouldn't, beginning with what Tommy'd do to us if he caught us, which is crush us like a couple of paper bags."

He ignored the warning. "Listen up," he said, lowering his voice. "First we've got to see if we can both fit inside the trunk at the same time."

"How're we going to do that? Tommy'll see us if we start fooling around with his car out here in the driveway."

"Here's how. After dinner tonight, tell your brother you'd like to practice driving up and down the driveway, the way he always let you drive his old car. When he lets you —"

"*If* he lets me," I interrupted. "He's only driven it a few times himself."

"Okay," said Silver. "If he says no, we'll just have to open the trunk and climb in out here. Maybe he won't go anywhere 'til after dark."

"Suppose he does give me the keys," I said. "What do I do then?"

"Drive up and down the driveway a few times to avoid suspicion. Then pull it into the garage and close the door behind you. I'll be waiting for you there. If we both fit inside the trunk, we're all set."

"Not quite," I said doubtfully. "He's sure to notice that we've fooled around with the rope, even if it is dark out."

"We'll have to take the chance," said Silver. "Besides, if he catches us right away, he'll just yell at us and tell us to beat it."

"You hope," I said.

"See you after dinner," he said.

"Uh . . . Silver," I said, stopping him. "This is a bit dangerous, isn't it? Hiding in the trunk of a moving car and all."

"Sure it is, Tramp," he said. "Getting up in the morning is dangerous, too, but that doesn't stop us from doing it, does it?"

He could see by my face that I wasn't convinced.

"We can't get locked inside," he said. "The trunk's broken. We'll be holding it down ourselves from the inside, so we can get out anytime we want." He paused. "Look," he said, "haven't you ever thought about what your brother and his girlfriend do when they're alone?"

I had to admit that I had.

"Well, here's your chance to find out."

"I don't know," I said, feeling confused all of a sudden. Excited and at the same time a little scared. "Anyway, we may not even be able to fit inside."

"Don't be so optimistic," Silver said, but before I could raise any more objections he was gone.

"It'll never work," I said to myself, secretly hoping that it would.

24
A Wild Ride

IT DID WORK, TO PERFECTION. WELL, ALMOST PER-fection. As I had suspected, Tommy hadn't given me the keys ("Let me get used to it a little first," he'd said), but that didn't deter Silver in the least. In plain sight, he untied the rope holding the trunk down, pushed me in, and climbed in after me, using the rope to pull the trunk back down in place. Then we waited, silently, in the dark, just long enough for my arm, the one beneath me, to fall asleep. Besides that, I was beginning to feel claustrophobic, worse than I'd ever felt inside Silver's bedroom hideaway. It was hard to breathe, and I was about to say something like "Let me out of here!" when I heard the back door slam and Tommy's steps coming across the driveway. The car door opened and shut, the engine roared, loud as a rocket, and we were on our way.

As we motored across town, Silver loosened his hold on the rope and a thin shaft of fading daylight and a cool breeze filtered into the cramped and suffocating trunk. My claustrophobic feelings lessened, replaced by other equally disturbing feelings. Somehow, sneaking around on my own brother didn't thrill me, whatever he was up to with his girlfriend, and never mind getting caught. And no matter what Silver said, riding in the trunk of a moving car was dangerous, in some ways worse than prowling around inside an empty house on Halloween or hiding wasps under the back seat of some thug's psychedelic car. Then there was Silver. What was the matter with him? He wasn't even friendly and he smelled bad, like an old rug left out in the rain.

We stopped for a traffic light in the center of town and Silver let the rope out even more, presumably to get a better look outside. A car, its parking lights on, pulled up behind us. I thought of how surprised the driver'd be if we just opened the trunk and got out then and there. But the light must've changed, for again we were off, passed by the fire station and Sally's house, all lit up (if only she could see me now!), the high school, the mobile home park, and a short way on into the country. No doubt about it, we were heading for my brother's girlfriend's house. We turned off the main road and onto a bumpy one, where my brother slowed the car down and hollered something out the window to a group of guys who were hanging out on the corner, smoking cigarettes under a street lamp. We sped up after that, took a corner at top speed, so fast that I sandwiched against Silver on his side of the trunk, and finally came to a tire-screeching halt.

The engine shut off, the car door opened and closed. I heard the jingle of keys and the sound of my brother's footsteps going up a gravel walk. A doorbell rang and a minute later a door opened. I recognized Ellen's high-pitched voice and laugh (who wouldn't?), like one of the harbor seals at the aquarium. The door closed. All was quiet, dark and quiet.

"Silver," I said. "Let's get out."

He was shocked at my suggestion. He loosened his hold on the rope and wiggled his body around so he could see my face in the light from a street lamp.

"Out!" he said. "Why?"

Given the opportunity, I shifted positions, giving my arm and leg a chance to live again.

"Don't you think we've come far enough?" I said. "There's no telling where they're going, or if they'll go anywhere at all. Maybe they'll just stay here."

"No way," said Silver. "Not with a new car parked out front, complete with tape deck, FM radio and all. Give them a chance. They'll be out soon."

"I don't know," I said.

He pushed his face nearer to my own. "What's the matter?" he said.

"He's my brother," I said.

"You mean spying?"

I nodded.

"I see your point," he said, "but . . ."

But he never finished. Instead he slammed the trunk back down in place.

"Silver!" I shouted.

He covered my mouth with his hand. "Shush," he whispered. "They're coming."

We hit the highway full tilt, and though I couldn't tell how fast we were actually going, back in the trunk it felt like about two hundred miles an hour. We sped along for a while, every so often going over a bump large enough to slam Silver and me around like a couple of pinballs. Silver was trying his best to hold the trunk down, but I could tell by all his grunting and groaning that he wasn't having an easy time of it. Too many bumps and a strong wind current kept tugging at the rope in his hand. Once, when we hit a particularly large bump, the rope was yanked free, the trunk flew open, and for a second I imagined our bodies flying out, smashing on the pavement, or being run over by another one of the speeding cars. Panic! When that didn't happen, I was sure that Tommy'd notice the raised trunk in the rearview mirror and stop to do something about it, but as luck would have it he didn't. Too preoccupied with his girl, I guess. Anyway, the two of us managed to grab hold of the flapping rope and pull the trunk back down on top of us.

Talking was out of the question, not unless we wanted to shout and risk getting caught. We couldn't hear Tommy or Ellen either. The engine was roaring away, and inside the car the tape deck was turned up full volume and blaring out music. I lay back, rested my head against the rim of the spare tire, tried to get as comfortable as I could, and wondered where the heck we were going. We'd turned off the highway I knew so well, traveled down some dingy-looking streets, past a crowded, unfamiliar shopping center, and onto another well-traveled road, where cars and lumbering trucks passed us on either side.

Then, just when I was beginning to think I couldn't stand it anymore, the trip ended as suddenly as it had begun. The car turned onto a narrow dirt road, flanked on either side by high wooden fences, slowed, and with a jerk came to a stop. Silver let out the rope a bit more so we could get a better idea where we were, but then quickly pulled it tight again, plunging us in darkness. Another car, its headlights blazing, had pulled up directly behind the Volvo. To look out now would've meant being discovered for sure.

Again, that awful claustrophobic feeling came over me. The darkness (where was Silver's flashlight?), the tight space, the car at a standstill — I felt as if a couple of hands had reached up from underneath the trunk, grabbed hold of my throat, and were squeezing the breath out of me. Hang on, Tramp! I told myself. Hang on!

I wiggled around, pushed my nose into a cold little air pocket, and tried my best not to think about it. I shut my eyes and listened: the idling rumble of the Volvo, the lowered music, my brother and Ellen's laughter, the honking of horns, and a strange echoing sound, like a whole lot of people shouting the same thing at the same time.

Bump! The Volvo suddenly lurched forward. Silver tightened his hold on the rope. Jerk! We stopped again. Bump! Again on the move. Jerk! Stopped. Bump. Jerk. Bump. Jerk. Bump. Jerk. "Oh, no!" I said out loud. "A traffic jam. Just what we need."

But it wasn't a traffic jam, for a moment later we rolled slowly forward, made a few sharp turns, and came to a halt. The engine and the tape deck were turned off. I waited expectantly for the doors of the Volvo to open, for Tommy and Ellen to get out, for the doors to slam shut. And then for Silver and me to get out as well — once and for all!

We waited — five minutes, ten — but the doors to the Volvo never opened. I kept hearing those strange echoing voices, nearer now and coming at us from all sides. With my free hand, I reached over and tugged at Silver's fingers, the ones which held the rope securely in place. He loosened his hold, just enough for us to get a look outside.

One look was all we needed. One look at all those shiny metal pipes sticking up out of the ground, the square speakers hooked on top, the movie star voices echoing inside, and I knew exactly where we were. So did Silver, who gave me an excited kick in the stomach.

Where were we? Why, at the drive-in movie, of course.

25
An Unlikely Predicament

"IT'S TIME WE GOT OUT," SILVER WHISPERED IN THE dark. He had his face pressed close to my ear and had spoken in the softest voice imaginable. So soft, in fact, that at first I'd thought it was my own voice whispering to me inside my head.

"Wait until I'm safely outside," he continued. "Then climb out as carefully as you can. No sudden movement. Tommy'll feel the car shake if you do."

Once more, Silver loosened his hold on the rope. Only this time he let it slide up all the way. The trunk was raised as far as it would go. I thought to myself: One look by Tommy or Ellen out the rear window now and we're done for.

Slowly, almost imperceptibly, Silver began to climb out. First he lowered his knapsack, then his legs, over the side, pushed forward, and with a soft thud landed on the ground. "Come on," he whispered. "All clear."

I tried to move, but couldn't. One side of me was all right, the one on top all this time. It was my underneath side that was giving me the problem — I'd lost all feeling in my arm and leg. Try as I might, I couldn't push myself up off the floor of the trunk.

"Come on!" Silver said.

"I can't," I whispered. "My arm and leg are dead."
Silver whistled impatiently through his teeth. Then,
without so much as a word of warning, he grabbed my
free arm, gave a tug, and yanked me free, clear of the
trunk and right down on top of him. Oooff! A miracle
that no car doors flew open, but it seemed that neither
Tommy nor Ellen had felt or heard a thing.

Silver was full of business. Shoving me aside, he
quickly got to his feet, took up one end of the rope and
pulled the trunk closed. While he was working on the
knot, I took a good look at our surroundings.

We were at the drive-in, all right, with about a thousand other people. The place was packed. Lucky for us,
Tommy had parked way over against a fence in the
back, the very last row. A road leading to an exit bordered us on one side, a long row of cars the other. In the
near distance, a giant, brilliantly lit screen was showing
some horror movie, a vampire sucking the blood from
one of its victims.

Gradually, the feeling began to ooze back into my
arm and leg. I crawled the few feet over to where Silver
was kneeling behind the Volvo.

"What do we do now?' I whispered. "I mean, how do
we get home?"

The light from the giant screen reflected a strange
gleam in his eye, a half-smile I was beginning to know
so well. Beads of sweat dripped off his brow.

"Is that all you can think about now?" he said em-
phatically. "Look around, we've hit the jackpot!"

"What jackpot?"

He looked at me to see if I were kidding him, saw that I wasn't, and said, "Don't you know what goes on at a drive-in movie?"

"I've only been to one once before," I said in a low voice. "About two or three years ago, when my parents took Ginger and me . . ."

He patted me on top of my head. "Tonight you grow up," he said.

All at once I realized what he was talking about — teenagers, boys and girls in back seats, doing who knew what! "Oh," I said, my eyes widening. "Oh!" I felt like a little-kid idiot.

Silver was beside himself with excitement. "Let's see what your brother and his girl are up to first," he chortled. "Notice you can't even see them up there. They must really be into it."

I grabbed hold of his arm. "Not my brother," I said.

He stared at me for a moment, then said, reluctantly, "It doesn't matter anyway. There are plenty of other cars. Just look at them all. And I'll bet at least half of them are filled with kids doing all sorts of things. Let's get a move on."

"Silver," I said, less excited than he was. Why I didn't know. "How're we going to get home? I don't even know where we are, what town we're in."

"The same way we got here," he said. "We'll come back later and get inside the trunk. But don't worry about that yet. There's a full night's work in front of us and not a moment more to lose."

Silver's "full night's work" consisted of doing only one thing: sneaking in and out of the rows of parked cars and spying on the people inside. As it turned out, this wasn't as easy as it seemed.

For one thing, we were only able to spy on the cars located in the back row and along the high wooden fences on cither side. Just about all the other cars jammed in the middle were out of bounds to us, because it was too easy to be spotted. We'd start peeking in somebody's window and before long the people in neighboring cars would be yelling at us, honking their horns, and otherwise making things impossible.

The parked cars near the movie screen were out, too. The light from the screen lit up the ground in front of it like it was daytime. Besides, there was a playground and a refreshment stand near the movie screen. Too many people, adults and kids, were moving about between the rows of cars, carrying drinks and popcorn and making what Silver had in mind difficult, to say the least.

Still, he was as determined as ever. At one point, after we'd been yelled at and chased away for about the twentieth time, he took me aside and said, "We're going about this all wrong. Let's concentrate our attention on the back row, except your brother's car. That's where the lovers park anyway, because it's darker there than anywhere else in the drive-in. Darker and more private. We should've started there in the first place."

"Okay," I said. "Only let's not let Tommy see us."

"We'll start on the opposite side," said Silver. "Come on."

We made our way along one of the high fences, keeping well back in the shadows, until we were once again behind the last row of parked cars. I had to admit, Silver had piqued my curiosity. Just the sight of all those dark and silent cars and the thought of what must surely be going on inside some of them made me as jumpy as boiling water. Already my heart was pounding.

The first car we came to, a station wagon, was a disappointment. Inside were a man and a woman and about ten little kids, half of them asleep. The second car was also a disappointment, and the third. So was the fourth, for even though two teenagers were sitting on the front seat, they were about as far away from each other as they could get and still be in the same car.

"Some date," Silver muttered sarcastically.

The fifth car, to use Silver's word, was the "jackpot." Inside, in the back seat, were two teenagers, my brother and Ellen's age, going at it like a couple of furnaces. They were kissing in a way I'd never seen before, certainly not up close, a kiss that never ended. Not for a breath. Not for anything. And boy did they squirm. It was enough to take my breath away. My heart was pounding right through my chest, my muscles — every one of them — were tight as wound springs, my clothes were soaked with sweat.

How was Silver feeling? All at once the breath inside him wheezed out like air inside an accordion. Startled, the two teenagers looked up to see our two faces staring at them through the window. "What the hell!" the guy inside the car shouted. At the same time, the people in the next car began honking their horn and shouting at us out the windows.

For an instant I was too paralyzed to move. The

driver's door flew open, smashing me on both my knees. The pain revived me. Good thing, because a guy the size of a polar bear jumped out of the car and began chasing me up and down the rows of cars, around the refreshment stand, and back again. He would've caught me, too, except that the movie ended, people in other cars began opening their doors, getting out for a stretch between shows, heading for food, whatever, and I got lost in the crowd.

Where was Silver? We'd decided earlier that if for some reason we got split up, we'd meet back at Tommy's car. I waited for a while, hiding out near the little kids' playground, until the second feature started. Then, staying as far away from the polar bear's car as I could, I made my way to the back of the drive-in. I was still in a daze from the night's adventures, when I discovered something else. Tommy's car was gone!

26
A Night to Remember

"HITCHHIKE," SAID SILVER. "IT'S THE ONLY THING TO do."

We were standing next to a busy road, under a large red and yellow neon sign advertising the double feature playing at the drive-in. In the reflected light, one side of Silver's face looked red, the other side yellow. I didn't have to see my face to know that it was green. I was scared and sick to my stomach because of it. My watch showed 10:30, a half-hour before I was due home. Hitchhiking, I'd be lucky to make it by morning. The thought of my dad waiting for me at the back door, or Tommy finding out what we'd done . . . Yeatch!

"Silver," I garbled. "We don't even know where we are. How're we going to know which direction to hitchhike in, what roads to take? Do you know what time it is? What if Tommy sees us? I'm not supposed to hitchhike anytime, especially at night. Do you know what my father's going to do to me? What happens if nobody picks us up? What happens . . ."

"Shut up," Silver said.

"Wh-what?"

"I said shut up." He put his hands on his hips and his face showed a look of pure anger. "The last thing we need is for you to go into your chicken-coward-baby routine. I thought hiding the wasps finished all that."

"What're you talking about?"

"I'm tired of leading you around by the hand," he said. "So cut the crap and use your brain to help me figure out what to do."

"But you're the one who got me into this mess," I said.

"Bull!" he said angrily. "You came because you wanted to."

"But my dad . . ." I sputtered, not knowing what to say.

"He'll be glad you're home," Silver said. "Which is more than I can say for mine."

"What?" I said, not sure that I'd heard him right.

"Never mind," he said. "It's none of your business anyway."

"Then why did you bring it up?" I said. But the moment I said it I regretted it. His face, which had begun to lose some of its anger, flared up again, red and yellow in the neon light. His eyes grew narrow, his mouth tight.

"You know what?" he said. "You'd be more of a man if you stopped hanging around that stupid girl all the time."

"Stupid girl? You mean Sally?"

"Who else?"

"Take it back," I said, giving him a shove.

But he didn't. Instead, he hit me, as hard as he could, right in my face, knocking me backward on the seat of my pants. Blood poured out of my nose and down my chin. For a moment I was too stunned to speak.

"So long, jerk," said Silver, darting across the street, avoiding the heavy traffic.

"You're just jealous!" I shouted after him. "Even Sally says so."

"A lot you both know, jerk!" he shouted back and headed down the busy street until he was out of sight.

It took me a moment or two to get my bearings. Then I stood up and wiped my nose on my shirt. The bleeding had stopped, but what was I to do now? It was either hitchhike or call my father. Hitchhiking seemed the wiser — or was it the more cowardly? — choice. If I were going to hitchhike, then it made sense to know what direction and road to take. About a block away a gas station still had its lights on. I could ask there.

See, Silver was wrong. I wasn't such a baby after all. Or was I?

After letting me use the bathroom to clean myself up (I could get the blood off my face and hands but not my shirt), the gas station attendant gave me all the information I needed to know. The directions back home weren't complicated after all, two main highways, and if I was lucky and got a ride right away, I might be less than an hour late. I hoped so, more than anything. If I could sneak into the house and get rid of my bloody shirt nobody'd ask me any questions. I might not even get punished. Maybe there was still a chance to get out of this mess after all.

The gas station attendant told me not to hitchhike on the busy road that ran past the drive-in, that the cars traveled too fast and that there were no good places for them to stop to pick me up. Instead, he told me to walk a short distance, climb an embankment, and hitchhike on another road, one that was safer and went in the direction that I wanted to go. I took his advice.

The road was long and dark and as straight as could be. Every so often a pair of headlights would appear in the distance and a moment later a car would come along, invariably slow down when the driver saw me standing with my thumb out under the street lamp, then speed up and pass me by. It was all very frustrating, and each time it happened (about fifteen times in all), the minutes kept ticking away and I knew the later it got the more trouble I'd be in. But what else could I do?

Finally a car slowed down and stopped a little way past me down the dark road. I ran for it, too excited and relieved to notice who it was. The passenger door swung open.

"Hop in," said my brother Tommy.

Ellen gave me a big smile and slid forward, pulling the back seat aside so that I could squeeze past her and into the back. In the overhead light she saw the blood on my shirt. Her smile became a frown.

"What happened to you?" she exclaimed.

"What do you mean?" I said, feigning innocence.

Tommy turned around and looked at me.

"Holy . . ." he said. "Look at the blood on your shirt. What happened?"

"Oh, that," I said.

"Well?" he said. The two of them kept looking at me.

"Are you hurt?" asked Ellen.

"Hurt? No, not at all."

"You're acting awfully strange, Tramp," said Tommy.

"I got in a fight," I said. "Couldn't we just get out of here?"

"With who?" asked Tommy.

I shrugged. For some reason I didn't want to tell them.

"Tramp's right," said Ellen, shutting the door, which automatically turned off the light. "Let's get going."

Reluctantly, Tommy turned back around, shifted into first gear, and eased the Volvo onto the road. Ellen slid over next to him and put her head on his shoulder. Even though I was in hot water up to my armpits, I couldn't help but think about the polar bear and his

girlfriend and the way they were kissing in the back seat
of his car. It made my muscles go tight all over again,
my eyes water. Good thing it was dark.

Ellen turned on the tape deck, but Tommy turned it
off.

"What brought you all the way out here, Tramp?"
he asked, trying to see me in the rearview mirror.

"Nothing," I mumbled, wishing that he'd just
shut up.

"Where's Silver?"

"I don't know," I said.

"What time were you supposed to be home?" said
Tommy.

"Eleven."

"It's past that now."

"Is it?" Once again I feigned innocence.

Ellen whispered something into Tommy's ear.

"There are a couple of T-shirts back there somewhere," he said. "Why don't you take your shirt off and
put one of them on? You're in enough trouble without
looking like a bloody mess."

I found one of the shirts and did as he suggested.

"Leave your own shirt in the car," he said. "I'll get
rid of it."

"Thanks," I muttered.

"Don't thank me, thank Ellen. It's her idea."

"Thanks," I muttered again.

Ellen turned around and gave me a big smile.

"When we get home, I'll tell Dad you were over at
Ellen's house with me," Tommy said. "You'll get in
trouble for not calling, but that's about all."

Now that's what I call a brother!

We rode along, got off one highway and onto another. Ellen turned on the tape deck, but I wasn't too interested in listening to music. I was too tired to be interested in anything and was glad a few minutes later when we arrived home.

"Thanks for the ride," I said to Tommy.

"Rides," Tommy said, as I squeezed past Ellen and out the door. "Make that rides."

27
The Return of The Spider Lady

A WEEK WENT BY, THEN TWO. LIKE MY RED AND swollen nose (I told my parents and the kids at school that I'd hurt it playing baseball), my anger at Silver subsided. Still, I stayed away from his house, almost until my own summer vacation started. I didn't even run into him accidentally. For all I knew, he could've been visiting his mother for the summer. I hoped that he wasn't. I'd be spending some time with Sally when she wasn't at her parents' cabin in the mountains, going there myself on occasion, but even so, summer would be a lot more fun with Silver and all his wild ideas and adventures. Then again, didn't he owe me an apology?

One night, after watching TV in the family room for a while, I headed for my bedroom and switched on the light.

"AIIIEE!'"

Never had I screamed so loud. There, plain as could be, was one of those enormous wolf spiders, its crusty skin brown and rotting on my clean white pillowcase. For a fraction of a second I thought it was alive, ready to spring at my face. I stood, wobbly-kneed, in the doorway, trying to catch my breath. Behind me, feet pounded down the hall. No doubt the rest of the family, minus Dad, who was away on a fishing trip, had heard my screams and were on the way to the rescue.

I don't know why, but I didn't want them to see the spider. An instant before they rushed into my room, I brushed the spider aside and put the pillow on top.

"What's wrong, Tramp?" my brother Tommy shouted. "You look like you've seen —"

"A ghost," said Ginger, a silly grin on her face, evidently pleased with her own quickness of mind.

Tommy shot her a look.

"Why did you scream?" asked my mom.

"Yeah," Ginger demanded. "Why did you?"

"Scream?" I said. "Did I scream?"

"Didn't you?" said Tommy.

"He did too," Ginger said.

"Yeah," I admitted sheepishly. "But it wasn't anything. I thought I saw . . . er . . . a hand sticking out from under the bed."

Tommy gave me a doubtful stare. Ginger looked impressed. She backed up a step and took hold of my mom's hand. Tommy bent down, lifted up the covers, which were dragging on the floor, and looked under the bed.

"Aha!" he exclaimed, startling the rest of us, even me. "Gotcha!" When he rose to his feet he was holding on to an egg-stained plate with a sock stuck to it.

"How awful," said my mom, giving me a look.

"Gross!" Ginger shouted.

"This wasn't what you saw, was it?" said Tommy.

"No," I said. "It must've been a shadow. That's it! A shadow when I turned on the light."

"Tramp, try to be a little more careful," said my mom, taking the plate and sock from Tommy. "You gave us all a start."

What could I say?

When they'd all gone (Ginger sticking out her tongue at me), I was out the back door and heading for Silver's house, the dead spider inside a paper bag in my pocket. Apology or not, this was too important not to follow up. A dead spider left on a lunchbox or a windowsill was one thing, on top of a pillow was another. The Spider Lady had been *inside* my bedroom, and I needed all the help I could get to figure out what, if anything, to do about it.

The door to Silver's room was open. I found him doing pushups on the floor.

"Silver!" I shouted, barging in. "You won't believe this, but ... well, here ..." I said, fumbling inside my pocket and retrieving the spider. "The most incredible thing ... The Spider Lady ..."

"Don't get all worked up," he said, rising slowly to his feet. "She didn't do it. I did. It's the same dead spider I found on my doorknob. I put it on your pillow while you were watching TV."

"You? But why?"

"It was as good a way as any to get you to come down here. Sorry I slugged you. Come on outside. You owe me one on the nose."

"Forget it," I said. "Why didn't you just come and get me? Or call me on the phone? Why all the mystery?"

"Oh, I don't know. Seemed like a good idea at the time. Come on, we're going outside."

"I don't want to slug you," I said.

Silver shrugged. Then a dazzling smile lit up his face. I couldn't help but smile, too.

"How loud did you scream?" he said.

"Loud," I said.

We both howled with laughter. It took a while to calm down, because each time we'd start to we'd look at each other's face and start laughing all over again. But finally Silver said, "Tramp, I've done some thinking the past few weeks, and I've come up with some good ideas for the summer, stuff that I know you're going to like, like going back to the abandoned house, for one thing. Sleep there all night if we have to."

"You're kidding?" I said.

"No, I'm not. And another thing —"

But whatever Silver was about to say he never finished. Cutting him off was a sound — a boom — loud enough for both of us to hear it clearly. At first I thought it'd come from directly beneath my feet, under the floorboards. BOOM! BOOM! A hollow sound, like someone pounding on an enormous bass drum. I started to say something, but Silver held up his hand. BOOM! BOOM! There it was again, only louder.

"The hideaway!" Silver exclaimed.

I thought he meant for us to hide and wait for whatever it was to show itself. (To my mind, a better plan would've been to hightail it out of there.) But what he meant was that the sound was coming from the direction of the hideaway. And sure enough, once we'd both crawled into the narrow space, the sound was significantly louder. Silver lit a candle, which threw a host of shadows about the tiny room. Boom! Boom! The sound, loud as could be, was coming from the other side of the wall.

"Let's get out of here!" I shouted.

"Do what you want!" Silver shouted back. "I'm staying."

I had no time to decide. As the two of us watched in utter astonishment, a tiny hole was punched open in the wall. A piece of plaster split off in a chunk and fell to the floor. It reminded me of the mud daubers beginning to poke their way out of their nest. Someone or something was coming through the wall, and there wasn't anything we could do about it — except run!

I scrambled to my feet, banging my head on the four-foot ceiling.

"Look!" Silver commanded. He pulled me down and turned my head toward the tiny opening. An eye had appeared. A bloodshot eye, with a dark pupil that bobbed about like a cork in a whirlpool. The eye fastened itself on Silver, hesitated, then shot a look at me.

Curiosity, for the moment, had overcome my fear. I stared back bewilderedly. The eye disappeared.

Suddenly there was one last tremendous CABOOM! And with a resounding crash the whole wall caved in. Plaster and dust flew everywhere. How the candle stayed lit I'll never know. Half the wall fell on my legs, pinning me to the floor. I pulled myself loose and made a frightened move to escape. Someone grabbed my ankle and held me fast. Gasp. I was choking so bad on plaster dust that I couldn't even yell for help. It turned out that I didn't need any — just yet.

It took a moment for the dust to settle. I sat up, rubbing my eyes, got Silver off my back (it was he who held my ankle), and turned around. There was the smell of sweet perfume in the air. And squatting like a wild-haired Gypsy in the midst of a pile of rubbish that had once been a wall, sat Mad Maddie, The Spider Lady.

28
The Night of the Tunnel

SOMETHING WAS WRONG. TERRIBLY WRONG. EVEN BY candlelight, I could tell that Mad Maddie had been crying. Out of breath from her exertions, she moved her head from side to side, seemingly bewildered. Where was she? Her whole body was shaking, making the single earring jingle about her ear. Her gray hair, covered by plaster dust, was matted down, wet, and sticking out every which way. She looked like a frightened animal paralyzed by a car's headlights.

Then all at once she lunged forward, took Silver by his shoulders, and pushed her speck of a nose an inch from his own. Her mouth flapped open and shut, but no words came out. Her small hands clutched at his shirt, tugging him forward.

"You want me to go with you?" Silver asked perplexedly.

Yes, she nodded, without speaking. Yes! Now that she'd made Silver understand, her face softened and two large tears began to roll down her cheeks.

"Through the tunnel?" said Silver.

"Yes!"

Tunnel? What tunnel? The word started me thinking again. Mad Maddie, of course, had gotten on the other side of the wall through a tunnel. The one that Silver had said had been built during the Civil War and since destroyed. It was obvious now that it hadn't.

"Yes," said Silver, "I'll go with you."

Mad Maddie was through the hole in the wall and into the tunnel in an instant. Like Ethel, her sister, she could move like a waterbug, crawling on all fours, knocking chunks of plaster out of the way with a hammer, the one she must have used to knock down the plaster wall.

"Get some help!" Silver shouted to me as he scrambled in after her. I should've done as he said, but I didn't. Something in the corner of the hideaway caught my eye. Silver's knapsack. How many times had I heard him say, "I'd be lost without it, Tramp"? How many times, in all the years we'd been friends, had its contents figured so importantly in our plans? "It's indispensable in times of emergencies." Talk about emergencies! Wasn't this one?

Without giving it another thought, I took up the knapsack, slid my arms through the straps, so that it rested squarely on my back, and plunged into the darkness of the tunnel.

I've heard that if you turn off all the lights in a windowless room the darkness is so deep that no matter how your pupils might enlarge your eyes never get — what's the saying? — used to the dark. That was what was happening to me. The farther I crawled away from the source of light, the candle in the hideaway, the darker it became. I could've closed my eyes and done as well.

Where was I? Where was I going? To do what? Had some calamity befallen Ethel? Had she been bitten by one of those hideous spiders? Had she somehow gotten her hand stuck inside the meat-eating plant? Had Mad Maddie finally gone bonkers and done something to her? Were Silver and I being led to the very same fate? Maybe the two sisters were plotting some evil revenge together. Yes, that was it! They were still angry at us for rushing out of their house, for rejecting their business offer.

"Silver!" I shouted in the dark, hearing the tunnel echo his name a hundred times. "Silver!"

"Uuuupppp heeeerrrreee!" came the echoing reply, farther away than I'd expected.

"Wait for me!" I shouted.

But no answer came, just a soft trickling sound. For the first time I realized that I'd been sloshing about in an inch or two of mud and stagnant water.

I hurried on, scrambling on my hands and knees, when without warning the tunnel took an abrupt dip. I slid forward, threw my arms out to try to keep my balance, failed, and fell into the water on my stomach and face. Yeatch!

It must've been the disgusting taste of the slimy water that brought me to my senses. Here I was stumbling around blindly in the dark, when surely the very thing I needed I was carrying on my back — a flashlight! Cursing my stupidity, I pulled it out of the knapsack and switched on the powerful beam. The tunnel lit up in an instant — three square feet, rocky walls and ceiling, with no end in sight.

I hurried on (no time to turn back now), passed the entrance to a second tunnel, and kept on going, hoping that it was in the right direction. It was. The tunnel continued to dip slowly, then flattened out. Didn't rats and centipedes live in tunnels? Had a family of spiders built a nest across the entrance? What a thought!

And then it happened. Up ahead I saw a light, a bright yellow light that became brighter the closer I got. In a moment I would reach it. But where was Silver? Where was The Spider Lady?

The yellow light, it turned out, came from Mad Maddie and Ethel's kitchen. A tunnel, straight from the crazy ladies' house to Silver's bedroom. Imagine! I fell in a heap onto the kitchen linoleum, behind an old bookshelf that had been pushed aside, along with a three-foot-square section of wall ("You've been through the moving wall again."), the entrance to the tunnel.

"Silver!" I shouted as loud as I could, but if he heard me, he wasn't answering. All was still, save for the metallic tick-tock of Mr. Bimbo and the distinctive crunch-munch sound of plant life growing up out of the dirt and soil, bit by bit.

"Ach, ach, ach, ach, ach!"

The stillness was broken by the sound of a racking cough — or was it laughter? — in another part of the house. I slid the knapsack off my back, hurried across the kitchen and through the swinging door into the dining room, the setting a few months before for one of the most horrible moments of my life. Before me, the polished top of the dining room table stood out in the moonlight, which cast a ghostly shine about the darkened room. One quick look was enough. In a far corner, hanging down from the ceiling, like a curtain, was a gossamer spider's web, intricate and wispy and inviting. Where was Silver?

"Ach, ach, ach, ach, ach."

"Silver!"

I ran through the living room, past the forest of potted plants, the spaghetti-eater still on the arm of the couch. Oh, please, don't let me see a spider.

"Silver!"

Feet sounded on the floor above my head. I took the stairs three at a time and found myself in a dimly lit hallway. Wasn't that the muffled sound of Silver's voice coming from inside one of the rooms? "Go back,

Tramp," the voice inside me said. "Go back and get help. Go back. Go back."

"Ach, ach, ach, ach, ach."

Suddenly a door at the end of the hallway burst open. A beam of light spotlighted me at the top of the stairs. "No!" I shouted, the knapsack falling on the floor at my feet. But it wasn't The Spider Lady or her sister or a hoard of long-legged spiders there to greet me. It was Silver.

"Tramp!" he cried out. "I've already called for an ambulance. Quick get your parents."

"Your knapsack," I said bewilderedly, remembering why I'd come.

"Knapsack?" He seemed as bewildered as I, more frightened than I'd ever seen him — or anyone. He shook his head roughly, his mop of silver hair flying all over. "Get your parents!" he implored. "It's Ethel. The ambulance is on its way."

Already I could hear the siren.

29
The Beginning of Something

THE WAY IT TURNED OUT WE WERE ALL PRETTY lucky. Ethel, after all, was over seventy years old. And when old people get sick with something as serious as pneumonia, they're just about cooked, if you know what I mean. At least that's what my mom told me.

The speed at which the ambulance arrived that night was astonishing. It flew by me as I was running up the street toward my house, shouting my lungs out. My mom met me halfway down the front walk in her bathrobe and slippers. When she saw me her mouth dropped open. Even in the light from the street lamp I looked awful — muddy, battered and bruised, and frightened. (She told me a few days later that I'd smelled as bad as I looked.)

"Silver! Ethel! The Spider Lady!" I blurted out the moment I saw her, and probably about a hundred other words that made no sense to her at all. But it didn't matter. The flashing lights of the ambulance parked in front of the crazy ladies' house told her all she needed to know.

She grabbed my arm and together we ran down the street.

Silver met us at the top of the stairs, in almost the exact spot where I'd left him. He looked as bad as I did, only everything was happening so fast that I barely had time to notice. He pointed to the door at the end of the hall. "In there," he said. He was shaking.

"Stay here," my mom told us. And with that she was down the hall and through the door, slamming it shut. For a moment there wasn't a sound, no racking cough, no voices, nothing. Then, almost before I knew what was happening, the door opened again, my mom came out, followed by two men, ambulance drivers, carrying a stretcher between them. On top of the stretcher lay Ethel, her eyes closed, her tiny face hidden behind a life-saving oxygen mask.

"She'll be all right," my mom told us. "A stay in the hospital, that's all."

The three of us went down the stairs behind the ambulance drivers, outside, up the stone walk, and into the street. Neighbors, some in bathrobes and slippers like my mom, waited by the ambulance, concerned looks on their faces. Mrs. Blanchard, who must've been staying at Silver's house, was among them. One of them, an older man I didn't know, volunteered to accompany Ethel and the ambulance drivers to the hospital. My mom told him that she thought it was a good idea. I wondered why my mom didn't go, too, but I soon found out. She knew enough to stay behind with Mad Maddie.

In less than a minute the ambulance, its siren wailing, pulled away from the curb and disappeared down the street. My mom explained what was what to the neighbors, Silver spoke to Mrs. Blanchard, and the three of us — my mom, Silver, and I — went back inside the crazy ladies' house.

Silver and I collapsed on the sofa.

"You two have had quite a night," said my mom.

We both nodded. We had.

"After I attend to Maddie, I'll make you some hot tea," she said. "Then I think the two of you should go home, wash up, and get into bed. We've all had enough excitement for one night. Tomorrow I want to hear the whole story. I'm sure it's a good one."

"Where is she?" asked Silver.

"Maddie? I left her upstairs," said my mom. "Let me go and make sure."

But she didn't have to. Mad Maddie was watching us

silently from the bottom of the stairs, looking a lot like Ginger when she's scared and doesn't know what to do. Her eyes were opened wide, her face and hair almost unrecognizable beneath a layer or two of dirt and plaster. She was still shaking, her earring jingling. I was surprised that we hadn't heard it. A trickle of blood oozed from a cut on the bridge of her nose. All this time, through the tunnel and everything, she'd been wearing her bathrobe. Of course, it, too, was filthy. Her bare toes stuck out the bottom like ten tiny worms.

Then it hit me, what she'd done. An old lady, crashing through a plaster wall with a hammer to save her sister's life. I couldn't take my eyes off her.

My mom sat down beside her on the bottom of the stairs and gently took her hands into her own. "Ethel's going to be all right," she assured her. "But more than likely she'll have to stay in the hospital for a while. You can stay at our house until she comes home."

Mad Maddie didn't budge.

"She won't go," said Silver. "She never leaves this house — well, almost never."

I had to give my mom credit. She tried. But no amount of talking could persuade Mad Maddie that to stay at our house was the best thing to do. She just sat rocking back and forth, shaking her head, no. She wouldn't go. Surprisingly, it was Silver who solved the matter.

"I'll stay with her, Mrs. Steamer," he said. "That way she'll have someone to take care of her and not have to leave the house."

I was shocked. Silver stay inside a house full of spiders, taking care of an old lady. The idea was ridiculous.

"A good suggestion," said my mom. I could tell that she was as shocked as I. "And nice of you, too. But if anyone stays, it should be me, especially tonight when she'll need someone to clean her up and put her to bed."

Silver hesitated for a fraction of a second before he said, "Then I'm staying, too. I'll sleep on the sofa downstairs."

The suggestion made me jump. Sleep next to the meat-eating plant! Ugh! What was he up to anyway — more investigating?

"That's not necessary," said my mom.

"Yes, it is," said Silver stubbornly.

Even if I didn't understand, my mom was beginning to. I could see it in the knowing look in her eyes, the way they softened, as well as her voice.

"You're on, Silver," she said. "I'm sure I'd enjoy the company."

"Then I'm staying, too," I blurted out, apparently suffering from extreme shock and amnesia.

"No, Tramp, you're not," she said. "We've all had a hard — "

But just then Mr. Bimbo began to wind itself up. "BONG! The time . . . is . . . eleven . . . eleven . . . eleven . . . o'clunk!"

I was instantly brought to my senses. Where was I? Why, in The Spider Lady's house, a place I'd absolutely resolved never to enter again. Sixty — or was it sixty thousand? — of those hairy monsters crawling up and down and all around, over walls and floors and ceilings, in your nose and up your pants, everywhere! No thanks.

For once, I was glad when my mom put her foot down and sent me home.

30
Secrets, Big and Bigger

SILVER'S BEEN ACTING STRANGE LATELY. TWO WEEKS after "the night of the tunnel," as I like to call it, and things still aren't back to normal. I'm beginning to wonder if they'll ever be normal again. For one thing, Silver spends almost all his spare time at the crazy ladies' house. It wasn't enough for him to spend one night there, the night Ethel got sick. He slept there every night for a whole week, sharing the sofa in the living room with the spiders and plants, helping my mom and a few other neighborhood people take care of Mad Maddie until Ethel returned from the hospital. He even went to the hospital to visit her. I know, because he bummed a ride with my mom and dad. And if that wasn't enough, now that Ethel's home and feeling better, instead of sleeping there, Silver has begun to spend part of every day working in their garden. That's right! He took them up on their business proposition, at three dollars an hour! The way he talks, I sometimes think he'd do the gardening for free, but then what do I know?

What Silver's filled me in on, that's what.

"The night of the tunnel," Ethel had come down

with the pneumonia she'd been fighting all along, coughing, wheezing, having a hard time breathing. The worse she got the more frantic Mad Maddie got (picture a little kid whose only parent gets sick in the middle of the night). To make matters worse, she couldn't use the phone or throw open the door and call for help — she was far too shy. She doesn't even go outdoors, not even to church anymore, except on rare occasions and at night, when she spreads around her dead spiders, large and small (good luck charms; it turned out that Ginger was right). Even so, the only way she'd leave or enter her house was through the moving wall and the tunnel her grandfather had built as an escape route for his family during the Civil War. Why she'd only use the tunnel was anybody's guess. Even Silver had no idea, and he'd asked Ethel.

Strange business this tunnel. Way back when, Ethel and Mad Maddie's family had owned both houses, Silver's and the carriage house (not barn) they now lived in. The tunnel had been built in a straight line from one house to the other. The main tunnel that is. There were two alternates (I remember shining Silver's flashlight on one) that ran parallel to the main and came out near the MacElvies' backyard garden. Silver showed me the two exits, small holes, both well hidden. It was through these alternate tunnels that Mad Maddie made her nighttime excursions.

Anyway, seeing her sister getting worse and worse, Mad Maddie did the only thing she could under the circumstances. She moved the wall aside and crawled into the tunnel. But this time, instead of coming up outside in her backyard, she went straight to Silver's house. She must've known that the plaster wall was there. Why else would she have brought a hammer? One thing is sure: she was lucky that the two of us were home. Maybe there's something lucky about spiders after all.

A week into my summer vacation, I found Silver where I almost always did these days, over at the crazy ladies' house, standing in the front yard, hosing down birdbaths and filling them with water. I had something important to ask him, but when I saw that he had his back to me I thought I'd sneak up and surprise him. He let me get about two feet away from him, when all at once he spun around, aimed, and doused me, head to toe, with water.

"Cut it out!" I shouted, leaping aside.

"Summer vacation just started and already you've lost your sense of humor," he said. "Pity. What's up?"

"Put the hose down and I'll tell you."

"I can't stop now," he said. "There's a lot more to do. But you're safe. I promise. Sit down over here."

I moved a cautious step closer and sat down on a stone step nearby. The sun was shining — hot, the birds were making a racket, and I could tell by the look on Silver's face that he was feeling different somehow, better. He was whistling, too, the first time I'd heard him do so in months.

"You mad at me?" he said.

"Why should I be?"

"Come off it, Tramp. For taking this job. I'm getting

paid, you know, my share and half of yours. You could make some money, too."

"No, thanks," I said. "As you know, I'm not too wild about this place."

"There aren't any more spiders on the loose," he said. "I've seen to that."

"I'm not taking any chances," I said. "How is The Spider Lady, anyway?"

He dropped the hose and stared at me. His whistling had stopped. "Don't call her that, Tramp," he said. "Ever again. Not Mad Maddie either."

My look of incredulity made him laugh. He picked up the hose.

"Eccentric is a nicer word," he said, imitating my mom.

"Sure," I said, laughing.

"Got a secret for you, Tramp," he said. "In fact, I've got two — big ones. But you've got to keep them to yourself. Okay?"

"Sure," I said again.

He fidgeted, yanked up a handful of grass, and shoved a couple of blades between his teeth. When he spoke his voice was soft, barely audible.

"Maddie talked to me," he said.

"She did?" I said, less surprised than I might've been. "Why you? What did she say? I thought she only talked to Ethel and little kids like Ginger and Betsy. And spiders."

Silver shot me a look. "I think it has something to do with trust," he said. "When you trust someone it's easier to talk to them. At least that's what Ethel told me. Remember the day we first met them and Maddie kept staring at me? Ethel says that's the first sign with Maddie. Most people she's afraid to look at — some phobia she's had since she was a little girl."

"About a million years ago," I said. "But why you?"

Silver shrugged. "Who knows?" he said. But I had the feeling that he did and wasn't about to tell me. Instead, he went over to the house and turned off the water spigot, then came back and stretched out on the grass near where I was sitting.

He said, "Maddie's set up a cot for me in a corner of the living room that I can use anytime I don't feel like sleeping over at my house. Sort of like being part of the family."

All at once he stopped talking. I had a better idea now why he'd punched me and said those things about his father and Sally; why he'd stopped taking care of himself and had begun to grin instead of smile. I also began to understand why Ethel and especially Maddie had taken to him, and, having befriended them, why Silver was beginning to look and feel better. I knew these things, but I didn't say anything.

"By the way," Silver said, "what brought you over here? Something up?"

"What's your other secret?" I said.

"The eye," he said. "The eye that I saw looking at me under the door, Halloween night. Remember?"

"How could I forget? We're supposed to go back and spend the night inside the abandoned house."

"We still can," he said. "For fun. But there won't be any mystery. I know whose eye it was."

"You do!" I exclaimed. "Whose?"

"Maddie's," he said. "I figured it out when she looked at us through the hole in the wall inside the hideaway. It was the same eye."

"Impossible," I said. "How'd she get inside the house? And why?"

"She's been following us around for some time," Silver said. "Keeping an eye on us." He laughed at his little joke. "You might say we're her favorites."

"But how . . ."

"She wasn't inside the house," said Silver. "Turned out the door I looked under that night led to the outside. She was outside in the bushes, looking in. Probably slipped in past the police when they opened the gate. She's capable of anything. Seventy-five years old!"

I could tell that he was impressed. So was I.

"What about the noises we heard in the basement?"

"Like the police chief said, rats."

The thought sent a shiver up and down my spine.

"Sally's having a party," I said. "I was hoping you could come."

"You're too late," said Silver. "She's already invited me."

I had to laugh. "I'll pick you up tonight," I said, getting up. Eight o'clock. Oh, one more thing. After all the trouble I went to, crawling through the mud and slime, scared half to death, did you ever use your knapsack?"

"Yes," he said.

"How? I'm curious."

The half-grin gave way to a smile. When he laughed I could almost hear the sound of bells ringing on an ice cream truck. "I knew you'd ask," he said, "so I fed the salami sandwich to the plant."

My friend. The Silver Bullet.